I'LL BE HOME WITH YOU

Finley Kaminska

For my fifteen-year-old self.

There is nothing in the world DJ can do that would surprise Jay.

Jay has known DJ for the better part of her entire life. She's known her through scraped knees and broken bones. She's known her through piano lessons and school plays and open mic nights. She's known her through first crushes and first dates and first heartbreaks.

The time before DJ is basically meaningless - most of it living in the vague, half remembered years of early, early childhood, the rest even earlier still. She's known DJ since it mattered to know people, and there is not a single thing she doesn't know about her.

Jay probably knows DJ as well as she knows herself.

Which is why, obviously, there's pretty much nothing DJ could possibly do that could surprise Jay. Not really, anyway.

Not that it matters at the moment, of course. It's early on a Thursday morning that's just like every single other Thursday morning since Jay and DJ moved in together three years ago. Jay is up first, because Jay is always up first, because her shift at the bookstore starts at ten and she likes to get a head start on the day. She's in the kitchen, puttering her way through her morning routine.

She is still in pajamas, her one actual set of pajamas with a top and bottom that match, because it's absolutely still seasonally appropriate for pajamas with blue snowflakes all over them and they're *warm*. Her feet are bare and freezing; their kitchen floor is currently doing its best impression of an ice rink. She can hear the radiators running, but they haven't yet made a dent in the winter chill bleeding through the hardwood.

Jay has just about decided that it feels like a pancake kind of day, blowing her bangs away from her eyes as she starts getting ingredients out. Pancakes are relatively easy - she and DJ are in the habit of putting dry mix together from scratch whenever they run out, so it's just a question of measuring it out and mixing in the wet ingredients. Jay could probably do this in her sleep. Which, given how heavy her eyelids still feel, is not that far off of what she's doing now.

It's all routine, built firmly into the way Jay moves through the world now. Measure dry ingredients, measure wet ingredients, mix but not too much. Get the skillet out, because they broke the electric griddle a few weeks ago. She starts the kettle as she stirs the batter together, but *this* she always gets wrong. It's almost like timing the tea wrong for having it ready at the same time as the food has become part of the routine, too, something she won't ever get right because she's built in the wrong habits. That's what DJ would say, anyway, if DJ were up.

(DJ would be right about that, Jay thinks, which is probably why Jay had the thought in the first place. After twenty years of friendship, DJ has firmly wormed her way into the fabric of Jay's thinking.)

It's quiet; the only sound in the apartment is the creaking of the kitchen floor as Jay moves around, the occasional clatter of utensil against bowl against skillet. Jay doesn't usually like the quiet very much, preferring to fill the air with some kind of talk or sound or *something*, but there's something about these early mornings that tends to bring out her quieter side. Maybe it's just that she's reluctant to wake DJ before DJ wakes up on her own - and DJ always does eventually wake up on her own, especially if Jay is making actual food for breakfast in place of just pouring out a bowl of cereal and having done with it.

DJ's a bad sleeper, though, and Jay doesn't want to be the thing that wakes her when she's actually managed to get some decent shut-eye.

Sure enough, though, she is starting to hear movement from DJ's bedroom. That she takes as a cue that it's safe to start making a little bit more noise - specifically in the form of humming a bit to herself. Nothing particularly groundbreaking or anything, just a song that's been stuck in her head. And if that song is maybe one of DJ's, it really shouldn't come as a surprise to anyone.

Jay is the first audience to all of DJ's songs, after all. She always has been, and she takes no small amount of pride from that. When they were in college, DJ would compose her new songs in secret, waiting for Jay to visit to let someone else hear them for the first time, and nowadays it's even easier since they live together; she'll play for Jay as she works them out. Jay writes them with her sometimes, now. This morning's is an old one, though, one Jay associates with the summer after their freshman year of high school and lazy afternoons spent in her parents' back yard.

She barely even notices the sound of DJ's bedroom door opening, and doesn't look up even when she does notice the change. She's got pancakes to worry about, after all. She knows from long experience that if she loses focus, she'll burn breakfast.

It isn't really until DJ starts humming along - or, more accurately, humming the harmony line - that Jay really registers that her roommate has joined her in the kitchen.

Still, she isn't surprised.

Nothing DJ does surprises Jay, because Jay *knows* DJ. Knows her well enough to know without turning around that she's wearing some oversized t-shirt and gym shorts as pajamas, that she's probably got some faraway look in her eye as she plans through her day in her mind, that she's hopped up to sit on the opposite counter to watch Jay cook.

Sure enough, when Jay turns to pass her a plate with the first three pancakes of the day stacked on it, there she is exactly as Jay imagined. The shirt has a faded image of their high school mascot Charmen the Chameleon on it, the shorts might actually be Jay's, and she's got this fuzzy distant look on her face as she takes the plate. She rests it on her thighs as she waits for Jay to finish making her own food. It's carefully balanced so the pancakes don't slip off, because DJ has her own familiar pattern and routine for mornings like this.

"Morning, Jazzy-Jay," DJ says, her voice a little rough around the edges from sleep. There's a flicker of warmth in Jay's chest at the sleepy smile that DJ is giving her, but that's familiar, too.

"Morning Dinah-binah," Jay replies, sing-song. Now that they've started talking, she splits her attention a little more evenly, turning back and forth from the stovetop to DJ.

"You made pancakes," says DJ, still smiling softly.

"I did do that," says Jay. "Observational skills still kicking in there, Deej?"

"Not all of us have been up for an hour already," DJ says. She rolls her eyes, then flips the end of her braid over her shoulder. "You're lucky I'm forming full sentences already."

Jay laughs. "Counting my blessings, got it."

DJ kicks her feet against the lower cabinets, her heels making a low thudding noise against the wood. She keeps a steady hand on her plate, though, resting on her thighs.

"Thank you for pancakes," DJ says. "I knew I kept you around for a reason, you freakish morning person you."

"Here's me, thinking it's because we're best friends," Jay says, laughing. "Twenty years of friendship are nothing compared to my ability to make pancakes while half asleep first thing in the morning."

"See, I knew you'd understand," says DJ. Jay finishes her own pancakes, and the two of them move to their dinky little kitchen table with their plates, the tea still not yet ready. "You're good for so many things, Jazzy. Noticing things when they fall on the floor -"

"Because I'm short?" Jay guesses, raising an eyebrow. Never mind that Jay is almost spot-on average height, even though DJ is five inches taller than her. That's on DJ being tall, not the other way around.

"Because you're short," DJ confirms, nodding. Because of course. Especially this sleepy, there wasn't really another angle DJ would've taken - she's extra predictable when she's tired. "And making breakfast, and writing words that make me want to sing. All good reasons, really."

"Oh, yeah?" says Jay with a laugh. That flickering warmth intensifies, warming Jay all the way down to her toes.

"Yeah!" says DJ. She grins over her pancakes at Jay. Something in her expression changes, and Jay can't quite put words to how, but then she goes, "Well, and I love you. That's a factor."

The kettle clicks off. There's a bang from one of the bedroom radiators. Jay's fork clatters against her plate - she's dropped it, but she barely even notices.

DJ is smiling at Jay, and it feels *different*. Her words hang in the air between them.

Time stops.

One: 20 & 18 Years Ago

(20 Years Ago)

It was the very first day of kindergarten, and Jay - then Jasmine - was *nervous*. She went to Pre-K at a different school, and what if everybody here already had friends and nobody wanted to talk to her and -

Most of her worries were gone by snack time. Sure, some of the other kids were already friends, but Jasmine wasn't having any trouble making her own. She really liked the kids at her table, which she figured was pretty lucky since they were going to be sharing for at least a little while. They were a table of four - two boys and two girls.

Straight across from Jasmine was Spencer. He had dark skin and short hair and the thickest glasses Jasmine had ever seen in her entire life. He told them he was nearsighted, and then explained that that meant that he was really bad at seeing stuff more than a little way in front of him.

"I got new glasses for school," he said, grinning widely. "I like them a lot. They're pretty neat, huh?"

"Yeah!" Jasmine agreed brightly. "I've never seen orange glasses before."

"I got to pick them out," said Spencer. "I've had glasses since as long as I can remember, but this is the first pair of *big kid* glasses I've ever had. I've never gotten to choose my own before."

"They're real cool," said the boy next to Jasmine.

His name was Isaac. He had a chipped front tooth and wide brown eyes, and he said he was a twin. Specifically, he told them that his twin was the reason he had a chipped tooth, because of a fight they'd had over a hard plastic toy when they were littler.

"My brother's in the other class," Isaac said brightly. "We've never been in different classes before. In preschool and daycare and stuff me and Mitchell were always together."

"Are you nervous?" asked Jasmine, noticing the little crinkle between his eyebrows that almost made it look like he was frowning, even though he had a smile on. "About being in different classes?"

"Nah," said Isaac. Jasmine was pretty sure he was lying.

"I am," the other girl at their table said softly. "My sister's in the other class, too."

Her name was Dinah, and this was the most Jasmine had heard her talk all day. She had long, curly brown hair, tied into neat pigtails that made little clouds of curls behind her ears.

"Woah, hey, are you a twin, too?" said Isaac, showing off his chipped tooth in a wide smile. He reached out for a high-five. "Twinsies!"

Dinah giggled. "Yeah."

"Don't be nervous," Jasmine said. "We'll have all kinds of fun, I bet. You won't even notice your sister's gone."

"If you say so," said Dinah.

"My big brother is in the grade above us, and he told me kindergarten is super fun," said Jasmine, patting Dinah's hand across the table. "It'll be good, I promise."

Dinah gave her a nervous little close-mouthed smile for her efforts.

Dinah looked a lot more worried than Jasmine had been this morning. Jasmine decided right then and there that she and Dinah were going to be friends, because it seemed an awful lot like Dinah needed one. She started making a plan to win Dinah over.

She was currently planning to see if she could convince Dinah to play with her for a while, and show her how super cool it was to not have her sister in the class because it meant she could make all kinds of cool new friends all by herself. And if that didn't work, her mom had packed her a mandarin orange for snack, and Jasmine was super good at sharing. Nobody could say no to orange segments, right?

A little later, their teacher declared it "Choice Time" and said that they could spread out across the room and play for a while doing whatever they'd like. Jasmine decided that this was a perfect time to put her plan into motion.

"Hey! Deenie!" she said, waving to Dinah. "Do you wanna play blocks with me?"

Dinah wrinkled her nose. "What did you call me?"

"Deenie," said Jasmine. She shifted to sit on her heels. "It's a nickname. Is that okay?"

"Uh," Dinah said, clearly thinking it over, "yeah, okay. If I can give you one."

Jasmine shrugged. "Sure, if you want. Do you want to play blocks?"

Dinah hummed, looking Jasmine over. "Sure, Jazzy."

Jasmine beamed. It seemed like, so far, her plan was working pretty gosh darn well. Dinah sat down next to her on the floor, reaching for some blocks. Dinah was really good at blocks, it turned out. She liked stacking them in ways that looked like they were going to fall over but never seemed to do it, and she showed Jasmine how to cheat at gravity.

While they played, they talked. Jasmine learned that Dinah's sister's name was Dahlia and Dinah was four and a half minutes older than her, learned that there was a piano in Dinah's house and she was going to start learning how to play it this winter, learned the difference between *fraternal* and *identical* twins. (Dinah and Dahlia were fraternal, but they learned later that Isaac and his brother Mitchell were the identical kind.)

In turn, Jasmine told Dinah that she had an older brother named Nolan and a little sister named Meggie, that she didn't know piano but she did already know all her letters, that her hair was long now but she was determined to cut it short-short one day.

When Choice Time ended and their teacher called them all to the rug, Dinah sat down next to Jasmine without her even having to suggest it.

Jasmine grinned at Dinah.

Dinah grinned at Jasmine.

It occurred to Jasmine, as she listened to their teacher read a picture book to the class, that that was the first time she'd seen Dinah really, truly smile. It made Jasmine really happy to see it - that her quiet, nervous new friend was starting to feel better. That *she'd* been the one to win that smile.

She decided right then and there that she wanted to make Dinah smile like that every single day.

(18 Years Ago)

When Dinah and Jasmine were seven years old, Dinah's mom had a baby. Jasmine had a playdate with Dinah about a week after the baby was born, and Dinah's mom let Jasmine meet him before they ran off to go play.

"What's his name?" Jasmine asked quietly, looking down at his teeny tiny face.

"David," Mrs. Jennings replied. "Would you like to hold him, Jasmine?"

"Can I?" said Jasmine.

"For a little while," Mrs. Jennings said. "He's in a good mood right now, so this is a good time for it."

"Thank you," Jasmine said politely.

"Sit down on the couch," said Mrs. Jennings. "Dinah, can you show Jasmine how to hold her arms?"

Jasmine climbed up onto the couch next to Mrs. Jennings, and Dinah climbed up next to Jasmine and started arranging her hands and arms so that when Mrs. Jennings passed Jasmine baby David she was ready.

Mrs. Jennings helped Jasmine support his little head, since he was too new to not be all floppy by himself.

"He's *so* little," Jasmine said in a near-whisper. David batted at her face with his tiny, smushy hand. His skin was smooth and soft and his eyes were wide and blue and captivating.

"Yeah, Jazzy," said Dinah, giggling, "he's a *baby*."

"But he's so little!" said Jasmine. She couldn't tear her eyes away from David's gummy smile. "He's got such a little nose and a little face and little hands!"

"You were tiny like that once, too," Dinah said.

"Nuh-uh, I was never *this* teeny."

"Were so!"

"Was not!"

"Were so!"

"Girls," Mrs. Jennings cut in.

"Sorry, Mama," Dinah said. She didn't look especially repentant.

"Sorry Mrs. Jennings," Jasmine agreed. She wasn't especially repentant either.

"Now, I don't know how big you were when you were born, Jasmine," Mrs. Jennings said, "but I'm sure you were around the same size as David is. Most babies are."

Dinah stuck her tongue out at Jasmine.

Mrs. Jennings sighed, exasperated. "Dinah."

"Sorry, Jazzy," Dinah said. She was even less repentant over this.

"Dinah and Dahlia were actually much smaller than David is," said Mrs Jennings.

Jasmine looked up, her jaw dropping. "No way."

Dinah and Dahlia were both taller than Jasmine by at least an inch. If Jasmine was around the same size as David when she was born, there's no *way* the twins were smaller.

"Of course they were," Mrs. Jennings said, smiling at Jasmine. "Think about it, Jasmine. They were *two* babies, sharing the same amount of space as David had."

Jasmine looked down at David again, then fixed Dinah with a skeptical stare. "That's crazy."

Mrs. Jennings laughed. "I suppose it is. Are you two ready to go play?"

Jasmine nodded, and Mrs. Jennings lifted David out of Jasmine's arms.

"Bye-bye, baby Davey," Jasmine said, giving him a little wave before Dinah grabbed her by the hand and tugged her down the hall and up the stairs to her bedroom.

Dinah flopped across her bed and Jasmine flopped down next to her.

"Are you excited about the baby?" Jasmine asked, laying on her back with her head hanging over the edge of the bed.

"Mostly," said Dinah, mirroring Jasmine's position. "He's real loud sometimes. Mama says that's because it's gonna be a while before he can talk, and the only way he can tell us he needs something is by crying." She wrinkled her nose. "I wish he'd figure out how to talk faster."

Jasmine laughed. "Meggie couldn't talk until I was in Pre-K."

"Oh *no*," Dinah said. She threw her arms up by her head

dramatically for emphasis.

"So, like, babies are weird and loud," Jasmine said, smacking Dinah's arm to refocus her. "You're in the big sister club now! Are you excited about that?"

"I don't know," Dinah said quietly. She rolled onto her side, scooting down the bed a little so she could pillow her head on her arm facing Jasmine. "It's really overwhelming."

"You think everything's overwhelming." That was true; Dinah had latched onto the word as soon as she'd learned what it meant. Fortunately, Jasmine was rarely overwhelmed, and the two of them were often together to keep each other steady. Jasmine rolled over, too, scooting onto the bed a little more to match Dinah's posture. "Why this?"

"It seems like a lot of responsibility, you know?" said Dinah. She chewed on her lip a bit. "I've got to set a good example and show him how to do stuff."

"You know how to do lots of stuff," Jasmine said, frowning.

"Not important stuff," Dinah insisted.

Jasmine sat up, holding a hand out to Dinah. Dinah sat up, too, and let Jasmine thread their fingers together. She put her other hand over Dinah's in her own, rubbing little circles with her thumb.

"You know how to *tie your shoes*," Jasmine said firmly. "You don't even use bunny ears."

"I told you I'd teach you," Dinah said, her brow furrowed.

"Exactly," said Jasmine. She squeezed Dinah's hand. "Deenie, you're so good at stuff. You can do big number subtraction in your head and tie your shoes and play jingle bells on the piano!"

"Is that important, though?"

Jasmine blew her hair away from her face in frustration. She kept asking her mom to let her cut it short, but mom said she couldn't until she was older, so it just kept falling into her face no matter how she clipped it back. "It's so important! *Deenie*, it's not your job or Dolly's to teach Davey, like, how to eat people food or hold his head up or walk. You've just gotta show him how to be a big kid, and you're the best big kid I know."

"That seems like an overstatement, Jazzy," Dinah said, uncertainty dripping from every word.

"Well, it's not," said Jasmine. She blew her hair away from her face again. "Meggie looks up to you more than she looks up to me, anyway."

"You're exaggerating," said Dinah, giggling.

"No, I'm for real!" Jasmine insisted. "Meggie looks up to Nolan, you, and me in that order."

"You're really silly," Dinah said, shaking her head.

"I think the words you're looking for are *you're really correct, Jazzy*," Jasmine said, her voice teasing. "C'mon, Deenie. You're gonna be the best big sister."

"I hope so," said Dinah.

"I happen to know so, just saying."

"I don't think this is a thing you can just *know*, Jazz."

"Well, I do. Deal with it." She blew her hair away from her face again. "Hey, Dee, do you wanna build a blanket fort? I bet it'd make you feel better?" And then she gave Dinah her best puppy dog eyes, because Dinah always fussed over the idea but she really liked being *in* blanket forts.

"Yeah, okay," said Dinah, with barely any convincing.

Jasmine did a little victory dance.

They set to pulling the sheets and blankets off of Dinah's bed, then setting up the chair and the pillows and the cushions they stole from the couch in the guest room down the hall. They made quick work of building the blanket fort, and then crawled in and cuddled up together in the little nest of blankets they'd built at the center of it.

"You're gonna be so good at big sister-ing, Deenie," Jasmine said, with her arms around Dinah's shoulders. "So good."

Dinah laughed. "If you say so, Jazzy. I'll take your word for it."

"You better," said Jasmine. "I'm right."

"Baby Davey is lucky he's got a big sister like you." Jay hummed thoughtfully. "And Dolly, I guess."

"Dolly's definitely going to be a good big sister," said Dinah.

Jay nodded. "I bet you both will." She squeezed Dinah again. "Do you want me to play with your hair for a bit?"

"Please?"

They shifted around so that Jay could comb soothingly through Dinah's hair with her fingers, braiding and unbraiding it while their conversation meandered into a playful argument over the merits of Goldfish crackers versus Cheez-Its.

They sat there in their blanket fort, talking aimlessly and playing with the dolls they'd brought into the fort with them and fiddling with each others' hair, until the sunlight filtering in through the sheets had faded into almost nothing. That wasn't saying much about the hour - it was midwinter, and the sun went down early - but for the fact that they'd built their blanket fort just after noon.

Before they knew it, Mr. Jennings was calling them downstairs for dinner and so that Jasmine could go home. By the time they make their way back down the stairs, much slower than they'd run up them earlier, Jasmine couldn't help but notice that Dinah's nerves from earlier had eased somewhat.

She'd even coaxed that warm, bright smile out of her best friend - the wide, shiny one that made Jasmine glow with pride every time she caused it.

After dinner, Jasmine bounced out the front door with a wave. "Bye Mr. Jennings, Bye Mrs Jennings. Bye Dolly, bye Davey! And Deenie?"

"Yeah Jazzy?"

"You got this!"

Dinah grinned. "Thanks, Jazzy. Bye-bye."

"Bye, Deenie."

Two: 16 & 14 Years Ago

(16 Years Ago)

They met Leo Cruz when they were nine years old. He'd transferred new into their school for fourth grade, and he got assigned the seat next to Jasmine's in class, because their teacher had decided it was best to alphabetize her students. He had sandy brown hair that curled just a bit at the ends, just long enough that it mostly hid the hearing aids tucked around his ears. He grinned at Jasmine when he sat down next to her, bright and easy with no hint of nerves.

She had a feeling that she and this boy were going to get along.

"Hi," Jasmine said to him as their class walked to lunch. "I like your light-up shoes."

"Thanks," said Leo. He took an extra hard step to show them off for good measure. "I'm Leo. What's your name?"

"Jasmine," Jasmine replied, wrinkling her nose. "But don't get attached to it, I'm trying to pick a new one."

"How come?" Leo asked.

"It's *so* girly," said Jasmine. "My mom says it's a kind of flower. I'm not really a flower kind of person, you know?"

"I guess," said Leo.

"She's spent the whole summer trying to come up with a nickname she liked," Dinah added. She'd been walking just behind Jasmine in line, but she stepped forward to throw her arm around Jasmine's shoulders. "We're still working on it."

"This is Dinah, by the way," said Jasmine. "Dinah, Leo. He sits next to me."

"Yeah, Jazz-*zy*," Dinah said, grinning, "I sit, like, right behind you. I noticed."

"I'm just *trying* to be polite," said Jasmine, sticking out her tongue. Dinah giggled.

"Jasmine Collins! Dinah Jennings! *Quiet*!" their teacher said from the front of the line, glaring back over her shoulder at them. Dinah and Jasmine both made appropriately apologetic faces, although Dinah didn't bother falling back to her spot in line. "We are still in the hallway, ladies."

"Sit with us?" Jasmine said to Leo in a whisper anyway. It was, at least, quiet*er*.

Leo smiled. "Sure."

The three of them claimed the end of a table together, and Mitchell flopped into the seat next to Leo's, introducing himself with a grin. When the other class joined them not too long after, Dahlia and Isaac claimed the seats next to their respective siblings.

"This is Leo," Jasmine said, having appointed herself ambassador.

She gestured across the table at him. "He's new. Leo, this is Dee's sister Dahlia and Mitchell's brother Isaac."

"Two sets of twins in one grade?" Leo said with interest, looking from Dahlia to Isaac to Mitchell and back to Dinah.

"Actually," said Mitchell, "there are three. But Maya and Marnie don't like us."

Leo laughed. "Alright. Sure, cool. Why not?"

"They're teacher's pets," Jasmine said. "And we're -"

"*Not*," Dinah finished, giggling.

Jasmine nodded. "You saw. We've already been told off once and it's barely halfway through the first day."

"Where'd you move from, Leo?" Dahlia asked, shoving her sister aside a little.

"Buffalo," said Leo. "We drove. It took *hours*."

"Oh man," Isaac said. "New York?"

"I don't know if there are other Buffalos."

"I bet there's one in, like, Wyoming."

"Why would he live in *Wyoming*, Dolly?"

"People live in Wyoming!"

"I'm from New York," Leo cut in, laughing. "Not Wyoming. Driving all the way from Wyoming sounds horrible."

"See?" Dinah said conversationally. "This is why teachers say we're a handful."

"I don't know," said Leo. "You seem like my kind of people."

Jasmine was inclined to agree. Leo fell in with their little knot of friends easily, which was a particularly good thing because he and

Jasmine kept getting paired up for projects in class, again due to their homeroom teacher's preference for alphabetization. He hung out with them after school and on the weekends, and in particular spent many cool afternoons that fall in the finished basement at the Collins house with Jasmine and Dinah.

"Why not just be Jazz?" Leo said, leaning back on the couch. It was October, about a week before Halloween. "That's not girly."

Jasmine shrugged. "I don't know, it just doesn't quite feel right, you know?"

"Jay," Dinah said, suddenly sitting up and staring at Jasmine.

"Huh?" said Leo.

"You should be Jay," said Dinah. She poked Jasmine's leg with her foot. "That's what Nolan used to call you, right?"

"Yeah, when I was a *baby*," said Jasmine. She wanted to dismiss the idea for that alone, but - "I don't know."

"I think it suits you," Dinah insisted. She reached over and grabbed Jasmine's hand, squeezing for a moment before letting go. "Not because it was your baby nickname. I mean. Just think about it, huh?"

"I like it," Leo agreed, nodding.

"Jay," Jasmine said, feeling how it fit in her mouth. It did feel sort of *right*, in a way that Jasmine couldn't quite articulate. "*Jaaaaay.*"

"Jazzy-Jay," Dinah said, sing-song. Leo grinned.

"Kinda rolls off the tongue, doesn't it?" said Leo. "Jay Collins. Suits you."

Jasmine hummed. "Yeah. I like it."

Dinah beamed.

* * *

Despite the new addition to their friend group - and Jay did very much enjoy spending time with Leo - there were still plenty of days that Jay spent just with Dinah and nobody else. Privately, though she would never tell her other friends so, those were always her favorite days.

One such evening came during winter break. It was the first time they'd seen each other since school let out, since Dinah's family had gone out of town for a few days and when they got home it had been Christmas and Jay's mom had said that meant it was *family time* and *church time* and not *go play with Deenie time*.

So now they were together, *finally*, hanging out in Dinah's bedroom because it was too cold to play outside. Cold but with *no snow*, which was a cosmic joke if Jay had ever heard one.

"I have a present for you," Dinah said excitedly once they got upstairs. She pushed Jay onto the beanbag chair under the window, then sat down next to her. She smushed in close - Dinah's room was always chilly. "I made it. Well, I decorated it."

She shoved a small rectangular object wrapped in paper with penguins on it into Jay's hands. Jay peeled the tape back carefully, because Dinah liked saving wrapping paper. When she had it fully unwrapped, she passed the piece of paper over to Dinah, who set it aside neatly.

The gift turned out to be a small, hardbound book of some kind. Jay was holding it upside down, so she turned it over in her hands. When she caught a glimpse of the cover, she gasped, looking up at Dinah's face. She was chewing on her lip, watching Jay carefully.

"You did this?" Jay asked.

The front cover was decorated with hand drawn stars and planets, all surrounding Jay's name which was written in Dinah's careful cursive with a sparkly gel pen. It showed a lot of care, the spacing of the planets, the swirl on Jupiter just like how Jay always liked to draw it. The impeccably neat curves of the *J-a-y*, ending on a little curlicue flourish.

"I did," Dinah confirmed, smiling nervously. "I thought it would be nice since you like to write and you didn't have anything with your new nickname on it yet."

Jay grinned at her. A warm feeling lit up in her chest, fuzzy and comfortable and pleasant. It felt almost like Dinah had lit a birthday candle somewhere in the vicinity of her heart.

"Thank you, Deenie," said Jay. She could feel her smile softening from her initial bright grin to something a little bit softer and warmer. "I really love it, it means a lot to me."

"I'm glad," said Dinah. She seemed genuinely uncertain of how Jay would react to her gift - as if Jay could ever dislike something so thoughtful. "I was a little worried you wouldn't like it."

"Are you kidding?" Jay said, hugging the notebook to her chest. "It's perfect. You know me so well, Dee." She set the book aside and tugged Dinah by the hands into a hug. "Thank you."

She held onto Dinah for a long moment, trying to convey without words how loved and known this gift made her feel. She had to do it silently, though, because she didn't *have* the words to explain it. She gave Dinah one last squeeze, then let her go. When Dinah sat back on her heels, Jay dug into her pocket for her own gift for Dinah.

"I've got something for you, too," she said, holding the little packet of wrapping paper out to her friend. Compared to the gift Dinah had just given her, her tiny gift seemed like almost nothing.

Dinah took it, peeling back the tape almost reverently. When she finally got it all unwrapped - it took a minute, since Jay's wrapping skills left much to be desired - the little necklace fell out of the paper into her hand.

She held it up. It wasn't anything special, just a little music note charm that Jay had made out of polymer clay strung onto a ribbon, but Dinah lit up like it was the best gift ever.

"Thanks, Jazzy-Jay," she said sincerely. "I love it. I really, really love it, I'll wear it all the time. Help me put it on?"

Jay nodded, shifting around Dinah to tie the ribbon neatly behind her head. It was a little too short to slip over her head, so Jay had taken special care to knot the ribbon on either side of the charm so that it wouldn't slip off when the ribbon was untied. She moved back to face Dinah, whose fingers came up to brush against the charm.

"It's perfect," she said, "thank you."

Jay smiled at her, and Dinah smiled back, and that flickering birthday candle warmth came back and didn't go away for hours.

(14 Years Ago)

"Hey, did you hear we're getting a new girl?" Jay said one afternoon when they were a few weeks into sixth grade. She and Dinah and Leo were hanging out in the Collinses' basement after school since for once they didn't have volleyball.

"Yeah," Dinah replied, stretching out and putting her legs on Jay's lap. "Dolly's supposed to be showing her around when she starts next week."

"How'd Dolly get picked?" Leo said, kicking his own feet on top of Dinah's on Jay's lap.

Dinah shrugged. "She's nice and also not a troublemaker like us."

"We're not troublemakers," Jay protested. "We're just spirited."

Leo snorted. "Yeah, I think that's the same thing, Jay-Jay."

"I don't *cause trouble*," said Jay, mock offended.

"No, but you always seem to be dragging me into it," Dinah replied, laughing.

"Offense!" Jay said, "I take offense! You talk in the hallways just as much as I do, Dee-*nuh*!"

"You always start it!"

"Do not!"

"Do too!"

"Like either one of you is actually innocent," Leo said, rolling his eyes. "You're absolutely not, neither one of you. I've seen the two of you in class, it's a miracle they let you be in the same homeroom anymore."

"I'm convinced they're afraid if they put me with Dahlia I'll corrupt her, too," Jay said with a wink.

"Well, that and that if we *weren't* in the same homeroom, we'd be causing trouble with you and the Garner twins anyway," Dinah added.

"It minimises damage if we're just allowed to be in the same room, I think. Not that we're troublemakers."

"We're just a handful," Jay agreed.

"And *that* is why neither of you got picked to show the new kid around," Leo said. He poked Jay's stomach with his toes. "Hey, DJ, did Dolly say what day the new girl is starting?"

"Uh, Monday I think," said Dinah. "DJ?"

"I'm trying it out," Leo said. "You need a nickname, Deenie."

"I have a nickname, you just used it," Dinah pointed out. She made a face at Jay, somewhere between amused and confused.

"If you hate it, I can call you something else," said Leo, shrugging. "I just thought, like, Deenie's your little kid nickname. We're *middle schoolers* now. Practically grown up. I wanted to shake it up."

"I don't hate it," said Dinah. "It'll just take some getting used to."

"What's wrong with Deenie?" Jay said, crossing her arms.

"Nothing!" Leo said quickly. "It's a nice nickname. I just thought it'd be fun to change things up now we're older."

"I like it," Dinah reassured him.

"No, yeah, I do too," said Jay, patting his foot. "Just don't talk down on Deenie, I gave her that one."

Leo laughed. "I *know*, Jay. When you were *five*. Anyway, this way you guys fit together, yeah? Jay-Jay and DJ!"

Jay grinned at Dinah. "I do like the sound of that."

"We can try it out," Dinah said, nodding.

The new girl did, in fact, start on Monday, it turned out. Dahlia walked up to their table at lunch time with a girl about Jay's height in tow. Her braided hair was swept over one shoulder, and she had sunny yellow earrings on that stood out against her warm brown skin. When she smiled nervously at the assembled group, she showed off braces with yellow bands on the brackets.

"Hey, guys, this is Lizzie Poole," Dahlia said, gesturing toward the new girl with one hand. "Her family just moved into town, please be nice and not weird."

"Nice and not weird, got it," Isaac said with an eyeroll.

"When are we *ever* weird?" Mitchell added, playing offended. "I'm not weird, Zac, are you weird?"

"I'm definitely not weird," Isaac agreed.

Dahlia sighed. "Yeah, great start boys."

Mitchell gave her a sarcastic salute.

"You've already met Mitchell," Dahlia said to Lizzie, "but that's his brother Isaac. Don't worry if you can't tell them apart right away, the teachers never can."

"Last year they switched classes for a day and it took almost six hours for a teacher to notice," Leo said, grinning. "They got in *so* much trouble, but it was the funniest thing I've ever seen anyone do."

"Thank you," Mitchell and Isaac said in unison, then high-fived. Lizzie looked amused, but also slightly baffled.

"I'm Leo, by the way," Leo said, waving. "I was new a couple years ago, so if you've got any questions about that give me a shout."

"Thanks," Lizzie said. "I might take you up on that."

"I'm Jay," Jay piped up, "and this is DJ. She and Dolly are twins, too."

DJ waved. "Hi. How are you liking it here, so far?"

"It seems really good so far," said Lizzie. "Everybody's been really nice, I think I'm starting to figure my way around. Dahlia's a good tour guide."

Dahlia grinned. "Thanks, Liz. I'm trying to be."

"Sit down," Leo said, waving at the open seats next to him. "We don't bite. Well, Dee and Jay -"

"Shut up," said Jay, rolling her eyes. "I thought we were not being weird, are you being weird right now, Leo Cruz?"

"I'm being weird, but I'm doing it with love,"said Leo. "I want Lizzie to know what she's getting into."

"Some nonsense," DJ said, directed at Lizzie. "You're getting into some nonsense. Don't let Dolly fool you."

"Hey, I don't have a problem with nonsense," Lizzie said, grinning.

"Then you'll fit right in," said DJ.

Lizzie and Dahlia clicked as friends right away, even beyond that first day, which meant that Lizzie pretty firmly joined their little group. And the thing about Lizzie being particular friends with Dahlia - bonding over books and playing piano but hating it - was that since Dahlia and DJ were twins, Jay ended up spending a lot of time in Lizzie's orbit even when they weren't hanging out with the rest of the gang.

Like this frigid January afternoon, when the four of them were camped out in the sun room at the Jennings house, watching snow fall.

It was their first and only snow day so far this year, and Jay and Lizzie had been invited over to take full advantage of the six inches-and-counting of snow on the ground outside. They were waiting until the opportune moment to breech the perfect blanket of snow over the back yard, knowing it would never be this pristine again.

"What are you *waiting* for?" David whined. He was only four, and his patience to this point was commendable. "I want to build a snow man before it gets too dark!"

"It's only eleven, Davey," DJ said in a soothing tone, smoothing over her little brother's wild curls. "We've got plenty of time."

"The sun goes down at, like, *three*, Dee-nie," said David. He batted her hand away. "What are you waiting for?"

"We want there to be enough snow for two good snow forts," Dahlia explained patiently. "*And* for snowballs, and for your big snowman."

David looked out the window, pulling a face. "I think there's plenty of snow for that."

"You know what," said Lizzie, taking pity on the preschooler, "I think there is. Let's bundle up!"

The four girls wrapped themselves up in layers, with sweaters pulled over their long sleeved shirts, extra socks layered over the ones they were already wearing, snow pants and jackets and hats and scarves and gloves donned. They all took turns helping David with his layers, too, so that the five of them could get outside as quickly as possible.

There's something almost magical about breaking through the first heavy snowfall of the season, flopping face first into the snow even though you know you'll regret it later or scooping up that first pristine snowball.

DJ, Jay, Dahlia, Lizzie, and David made quick work of destroying the perfect, clean sheet of snow that had fallen over the Jennings's back yard.

David was given one corner of the yard declared off limits for the snowball fight, a whole corner to himself to work on building a snow man as tall as he was. Jay was privately uncertain of his ability to manage that particular task, though that was what he'd set out to do and who was she to tell him he couldn't at least try.

The girls drew a boundary line down the center of the rest of the yard - the north half for Jay and DJ, the south half for Dahlia and Lizzie. Jay tried to tune out what Lizzie and Dahlia were up to, focused entirely on building her and DJ's fort while DJ set to creating a massive stockpile of snowballs.

She dug out a little hole, packing the snow on the sides as much as she could, and started building up a wall around it, facing Dahlia and Lizzie's side with an opening toward the fence so they could get in and out easily. By the time that she was satisfied with it, DJ had created an impressive pile of snowballs, which she'd stacked to one side of Jay's fort.

"We're ready!" Jay called, looking across the yard for the first time since she'd started working.

Dahlia and Lizzie's fort seemed to be of a similar design to theirs, although it was wider with a slightly flatter, lower wall, where DJ and Jay's was rounded and narrow.

"So are we!" Lizzie shouted back.

"On three!" DJ said.

"One," said Dahlia.

"Two," said DJ.

"Three!" they shouted in near-unison, and then the war began.

It was chaos - snowballs flying every which way, a few going rogue and landing dangerously close to David's snowman project, fortress walls under constant bombardment and in near constant need of shoring up and repair, fingers and noses and toes getting colder and colder by the minute, but nobody really caring because they were having entirely too much fun to notice the chill.

There was no way to really declare a winner, the girls just kept going until they were all exhausted and damp and freezing.

"You ready to go in, Davey?" Jay said, coming over to investigate his snowman project.

He was sitting back on a snowbank, admiring his own work. It was clear that an attempt had been made for a big snowman, but for whatever reason it had been abandoned partially finished off to one side, with tiny fistfuls of snow scooped out of its base, in favour of a field of knee-height snowmen. There were probably fifteen of them, all in various poses with bits of twig forming their facial features and limbs.

"Yeah," he said, grinning up at her. "I'm good. Was your snowball fight good?"

"Yeah," Jay replied, smiling back. "It was lots of fun. You need a hand getting up?"

David shook his head firmly, and scrambled to his feet.

The five of them trooped inside, leaving their wet, snowy outerwear by the back door.

"I've got hot chocolate ready!" Mrs. Jennings told them as they found their way into the kitchen one at a time.

"Thanks, Mrs. Jennings," Jay and Lizzie said, while the three Jennings kids said, "Thanks, Mom," at the same time.

"Did you kids have fun?" she asked. She passed each of them a mug, making sure to give David the smallest one.

"Yeah!" David said, grinning. "I built *so many* snowmen, Mama."

"I'll have to go out and see them," Mrs. Jennings replied. "Girls, how was your snowball fight?"

"Super fun," said Lizzie.

"Jazzy built the best snow fort we've ever had, Mom," DJ said. She smiled at Jay over her mug as she said it, which warmed Jay right up from the inside out. "It was awesome."

"Thanks, Deej," Jay replied. "You made some real good snowballs, too."

They high-fived. "Best team ever!"

Dahlia and Lizzie didn't even try to dispute it.

Three: 12 Years Ago

Jay was thirteen years old, and she had a *huge* crush on her best friend.

Leo, of course. She had a crush on Leo.

Her heart sped up when she could make him smile, when she could win his wheezy laugh. (Leo had a bad habit of forgetting to breathe when he thought something was funny, so his laugh always sounded like he didn't have enough air to make the sound. Always. Jay thought it was kind of charming.) She got blushy and tongue-tied when they had long conversations alone. That one was a bit of a problem, because Leo was her best friend save DJ, and as such they had an awful lot of conversations just the two of them.

"You're killing me," DJ said, throwing a sweater across the room at Jay. "You're *killing me*, Jazzy-Jay. Have you told Leo you like him?"

"What?" said Jay, startled. "No!"

"*Why?*" asked DJ. Her voice is dripping with exasperation and frustration.

Jay opened and closed her mouth a few times. "I can't just *tell him* that!"

"Why not?" DJ said. She rolled her eyes.

"He's our friend!" said Jay. "What if he doesn't like me and he thinks it's weird that I like him and he stops talking to us and our friend group deteriorates and everybody hates me forever?"

DJ snorted.

"I'm serious!"

"I know you are," said DJ. "That's kind of why it's funny."

"I don't appreciate you," said Jay. She threw the sweater back toward DJ. DJ batted it away easily. "I don't appreciate this kind of behavior from you."

"You appreciate me so much, you know why?" DJ replied. "I'm the only one who will put up with your nonsense."

"Nolan, Leo, Dahlia, Lizzie," Jay listed off, counting them off on her fingers.

"If you think that your brother wants to hear you whine about how much you like Leo, please *please* pitch that to him while I'm here. I want to watch him shut you down." DJ grinned at her. "Come on, Jazz. Leo's, like, your best friend - besides me, of course - he's not going to be weird about it. And I bet he likes you back, he'd be crazy not to."

"Crazy?" Jay echoed disbelievingly.

"Crazy," DJ confirmed. "I mean, think about it, Jazzy-Jay. You're funny and you're smart and you're really pretty, too."

"You think I'm pretty?" Jay said, tipping her head to one side. Not entirely consciously, she brought a hand up to her hair, tucking it behind her ear. Her mom had finally given in on letting her cut it, but only partway - a *compromise*, she'd insisted - so now the ends just brushed her jawline. That warm feeling in her chest is back in full force, warming her from the inside out. She might be blushing.

"Well, yeah," said DJ. She shrugged, waving across Jay. "You're - I mean. All the boys say so, I've heard them."

"I don't care about the boys," Jay said, shaking her head. "Well, Leo. But *you* think -"

"Of course I do," said DJ. "Did you think I didn't?"

"I don't know," said Jay. She combed her fingers through her hair again, feeling self conscious. "You and Dolly are all tall and pretty with your long hair and blue eyes and I'm just -"

"Short and pretty," DJ said firmly. "And you like your short hair, right?"

"Yeah," Jay said.

DJ reached over and pulled Jay's hand away from her face, lacing their fingers together instead. "Then that's all that matters. Anybody who doesn't think you're pretty just because you've got short hair is objectively wrong." She hummed, squeezing Jay's fingers. "You don't normally talk like this, Jazzy. Is something bothering you?"

Jay shrugged again. "You said it, I'm just - reacting, I guess. I don't know."

"Sorry," DJ said. "I didn't expect that it would upset you."

"I'm not upset," Jay said quickly. "I'm just not good at taking compliments like that, I guess."

"Well, you should get used to it," said DJ. "Because you're wonderful and you're beautiful and you're so smart, and I am not above telling you that every time I see you until you can take it without trying to argue with me."

Jay was definitely blushing now. "D-J. You don't have to be like that."

"I do," said DJ. "I'm your best friend, I'm contractually obligated to remind you that you're pretty on a regular basis. I've got to hype you up. Especially if you're going to tell Leo you like him, which you totally definitely should do!"

"I don't know about that," said Jay.

"I do!" said DJ. "What could go wrong, really? *Really*? This is Leo we're talking about, *Leo*. The worst thing that I could possibly fathom happening is that you'd tell him and he wouldn't like you back and you'd stay friends." She shook Jay's shoulder with her free hand. "But the best case scenario is that Leo likes you, too, and you put me out of my misery by actually dating him!"

"Put *you* out of *your* misery?" Jay echoed. "*You!*"

"Yeah, *me!*" DJ said. She shook Jay's shoulder again. "Who's got to listen to you moon over his shiny hair and goofy smile, Jazz? I'll give you one guess, because it sure as heck isn't Nolan or Dahlia or the Garner boys."

"Hey, you don't know," said Jay. She was laughing now, though, which made DJ smile. "Maybe I go over to Zac and Mitch's house on Friday nights and gossip about boys with them, too!"

DJ snorted. "Yeah, like Mitch and Zac would put up with that."

"You don't know!" Jay repeated, still laughing.

"I'll help you make a game plan to tell him, how's that?" DJ said.

"Deej -"

"If you really don't want to, I won't make you," said DJ, squeezing Jay's hand, "I would never do something like that. I just think you'd be happier if you just got it out there."

"Maybe," said Jay. "Maybe."

"Okay," said DJ.

That was the end of the conversation, more or less. DJ had to go downstairs and practice piano, anyway, and Jay trailed after her because she liked listening to DJ play and anyway, if she went home now she'd have to do something way more boring like help Meggie with her math homework. Jay always got stuck helping Meggie with her math homework, which was annoying, because Meggie should just get better at math and stop bothering Jay about it.

(Or at least Nolan should have to do it sometimes.)

So Jay nestled in the corner of the couch, the chunky knit blanket she liked wrapped around her while she listened to DJ. Well, listened and watched. For all that Jay always said she'd read or sketch while DJ practiced, she always ended up just watching DJ play, transfixed.

And could she really be blamed for that? DJ had been playing piano since they were small, and by now it came easily, muscle memory, but still looked just as incredible and impressive to Jay as it had when they were seven and all DJ could play reliably was jingle bells.

She relaxed into the cushions, enjoying the comfortable familiarity of watching DJ practice and mulled over DJ's suggestion.

She *could* tell Leo she liked him. DJ was probably right that he wouldn't be weird about it if she did, even if he didn't like her back. The worst that would probably happen would be that she'd be a little embarrassed, and she'd avoid Leo for a couple of days until she got over that and things would be fine afterward.

The best case scenario was that Leo liked *her*, too, and maybe they would - something. Date, maybe. Some of their classmates were starting to date, and that's what you did when you liked someone, right? It was all still sort of practice dating, of course, figuring out how to be around a person and all - dating someone in middle school wasn't exactly high stakes - but for thirteen-year-old Jay it felt a little overwhelming.

What was more daunting, she found herself wondering, the idea of being rejected, or the idea that he might like her, too?

She honestly wasn't sure. Living in this limbo of not really feeling prepared to tell him about it and not really wanting to keep it to herself anymore was kind of getting frustrating, too.

Better to have done with it, right? That way she couldn't worry about it anymore, even if she wanted to. She would have done it, and she'd have an answer, and even if Leo didn't like her she'd *know*.

And whatever happened, DJ would be there. She'd help.

Jay had always been able to trust that DJ would have her back, and this was really no different, was it? DJ had said as much, earlier. That she'd be right there backing Jay up or holding her together no matter what Leo said.

How Leo felt.

"Hey, Deej?" Jay said, leaning forward with her elbows on her knees, looking at DJ.

DJ stopped playing, looking back over her shoulder at Jay. "What's up, Jazz?"

"I want to tell him," Jay said simply. "Will you help me figure out what to say?"

"Of course," said DJ, smiling softly at Jay. There was a little flicker of candle flame warmth in Jay's chest at the confirmation that DJ had her back. "I'll always help you, Jazzy-Jay."

The scheme to tell Leo about Jay's feelings took approximately three weeks to set into motion, which was a lot of time when one considered that the plan ultimately came down to:

"Hey, Leo, I like you. Like, I *like*-like you."

"Oh, cool. I, uh, I kinda like-like you, too."

And that was really the end of it.

When Jay told DJ how the whole thing had gone down, she had laughed for almost ten whole minutes. And then her laughter had brought Nolan to Jay's doorway to investigate, so DJ had explained the whole thing to him through peals of renewed laughter. Which, of course, Nolan had joined in on.

Jay, her cheeks burning red, had just sat there and let the whole thing happen, because there wasn't much else to do about it.

So Jay and Leo dated, in the childish way middle schoolers "date."

There was a lot of hand holding, this being the primary way they expressed affection beyond their usual. Sometimes they even held hands at *school*, at the lunch table or what have you, but that always earned them an absolute avalanche of teasing, so they didn't do it often.

Most of the time they spent together was still with their friends, and they'd just sort of pair off on the side of the group. They went to movies with their whole crew, sitting to the end of the row and holding hands through the whole movie in the dark. They trailed behind the group as they walked to and from school events or between each other's houses.

The first time Jay and Leo actually went out *alone* together was a pretty big deal, a few weeks after they'd declared themselves boyfriend and girlfriend. It was a Friday evening, and Leo's mom dropped him off at Jay's house so that the two of them could walk together to the little frozen custard shop a few blocks down. They held hands as they walked, their fingers interlaced.

(It was a feeling Jay was still getting used to, holding hands like this. She was more accustomed to the more little-kiddish way of holding hands where you just wrap your hand around the other person's hand and have done with it, and the feeling of lacing their fingers together was new but not unpleasant.)

"You look really pretty tonight, Jay-Jay," Leo said, his cheeks a little bit pink.

Jay flushed, sweeping her hair over her ear with her free hand. "You think?"

"Yeah!" said Leo. He opened and closed his free hand a few times, like he sometimes did when he was at a loss for words. He'd told Jay once last year that it was because signs usually came to mind first - technically, English was his second language. "I mean, you always look pretty, but - I just - yeah. You look nice."

"Thanks," said Jay. She giggled, a little self-conscious. "My outfit was DJ approved. I picked it out and stuff, but Deej is better at, like, intentional looks and stuff, so I ran it by her."

"Well it's good," Leo said, with a little laugh of his own.

"Thanks," Jay said again. "I'm sorry, I'm being so awkward. I don't - I don't know what to say. We've been friends for four years and suddenly I'm at a loss."

Leo shrugged. "I know how you feel. It's like suddenly there's all this pressure on anything I say. Even though it's just you, and you're still the same you that you were a month ago. It's just like, that's Jay, but that's *Jay*. Girlfriend Jay."

"Girlfriend Jay," Jay echoed, nodding. She got what he was trying to say. "Boyfriend Leo. I feel the same way."

"Thank God," Leo said, sounding genuinely relieved. "I kind of thought it was just me. You're all - well, you're pretty collected, Jay-Jay."

"Oh, it's a very thin veneer," said Jay, "pasted hastily over how much I panicked over telling you I liked you. Did I tell you about that? God, I swear I've been mooning over you to Nole and Deej for months now, and DJ finally got fed up with me and convinced me to tell *you* about it."

"Well, I'll have to thank DJ, then," said Leo. He grinned at her, squeezing her hand. "Since if she hadn't I don't know if we'd have gotten here. I've been doing the same thing to Zac and Mitch and I think they were planning to, like, murder me in my sleep over it if I didn't get over myself soon."

Jay snorted. "Boys. I'm glad they didn't, or I wouldn't be on this lovely walk with you."

"A lovely walk that is going to end in ice cream, which is even better."

"Custard, Leo. Custard."

"They're the same thing."

"They absolutely are not. We may have to break up over this."

Leo laughed, that full, wheezy laugh that Jay found so charming. "Oh, over this?"

"It's an important difference!" Jay insisted, but she was laughing, too.

They arrived at the shop before things could devolve any further, and ordered their custard. They claimed a table along the wall to eat at, sitting facing each other. Jay had her back to the wall, facing out, but despite the bustling shop with interesting decorations full of distractions, she really only had eyes for Leo.

It was a nice evening. Leo had gotten butterscotch custard, which Jay thought was a little bit ridiculous when there was chocolate *right there*, and she let him know that. With the ice having been broken on their walk over, it felt a lot more normal. A lot more like talking to Leo, her second best friend in the world, than Leo, the boy she was on her very first date ever with.

They walked back to Jay's house together, holding hands again. Leo swung their hands between them as they walked. His mom was coming back to pick him up soon, and they sat on Jay's front porch and waited for her.

In the in-between time, after they'd gotten back but before his mom arrived, Leo leaned over and gave Jay a very tentative kiss on the cheek.

It was clumsy and unpracticed and new, but Jay felt her heart flutter in her chest and her cheeks flush bright red anyway.

Leo was Jay's first proper kiss, too, in the stairs behind the stage at their middle school musical. It was right before the first night's show, and he'd followed it with a mumbled, *"Break a leg, Jay-Jay,"* before disappearing into the wings, red faced.

Jay had been left on the bottom step of the stairwell, one hand coming up to her mouth almost unconsciously. DJ found her there not long after, and she'd taken one long look at Jay before giving her a knowing smile and tugging her by the arm backstage. No time for shock when it's places call, anyway.

They dated until almost April, by far the longest and steadiest relationship in their eighth grade class. In the end, it was Leo who broke it off.

"I don't -" He flexed his fingers a few times, searching for words. "I think we should just be friends, Jay-Jay. The end of the year and, like, starting high school is - it's a lot. I don't want to lose your friendship by putting the strain of trying to date on top of all of that."

Jay nodded. "Yeah, I - yeah. You're right."

"Sorry."

"Yeah, me too."

And then she went to DJ's house after school and cried. It wasn't the end of the world by any means, but it still stung. The end of her first relationship - her very first breakup. DJ held her until she'd cried herself out, the two of them curled up together at the head of DJ's bed under the chunky knit blanket Jay liked that usually lived on the couch by the piano.

While Jay cried, DJ ran her fingers soothingly through her hair, humming aimlessly. She didn't try to tell Jay it was okay - it wasn't, and that was allowed - and she didn't tell her that she'd feel better eventually - she knew that. She just sat there and let Jay process the whole thing, and then they could move on with their lives afterward.

Jay appreciated that about DJ; she'd known Jay long enough to know what she needed to hear, and more importantly, to know when to just be quiet with her.

"Thanks, Deenie," Jay said when she was feeling a little bit better.

"Of course, Jazzy-Jay," said DJ.

(Jay had a moment, then, of quiet appreciation for the fact that there was nobody besides Leo who called her Jay-Jay. She felt like that nickname would probably sting for a while.)

"Do you want to listen to me play for a bit?" DJ suggested. At Jay's nod, she slipped out of Jay's grip and moved to grab her guitar. It was relatively new, she was still learning, but Jay still loved hearing her practice.

Jay and Leo were okay eventually, of course. They were thirteen and fourteen, and middle schoolers are generally sturdy when it comes to things like that. It took a little while, a little bit of walking on eggshells, but by the beginning of freshman year they were thick as thieves again, like nothing had ever changed.

Four: 11 Years Ago

They met Eleanor "Call Me Nell" Rask on their high school freshman orientation day. She was in their homeroom, and lined up next to DJ for school pictures. She had this *cloud* of white-blond curls floating around her face, clipped back on one side with a snap clip while the other side fell into her eyes. She spent the whole day batting the loose side away from her face halfheartedly while she talked.

"I like your necklace," she said to Jay, leaning around DJ to talk while they waited for photos. "I've never seen one like that."

Jay touched the necklace sort of automatically, even though she remembered clearly which one she'd put on. It was a little string of beads that she'd painted to look like the planets, separated by dangly beads shaped like tiny stars. "Thanks."

"She made it," DJ cut in when it became clear Jay wasn't going to say so. "Isn't it awesome?"

"It's not that big a deal, Deej," Jay said, blushing a little. There was a little flare of warmth in her chest even though she was a tiny bit embarrassed.

"Wait, really?" said Nell. "That's so cool!"

"The coolest," DJ agreed, grinning and throwing an arm around Jay's shoulders. "Jay's real talented with fiddly stuff like that."

"Thanks, DJ," said Jay. She knew better than to argue the point.

"Do you like space a lot?" Nell said brightly. "I love space, it's fascinating."

That turned into a conversation about space travel which turned into an argument about aliens that carried them through the end of the half-day of orientation. That afternoon, while they stood on the sidewalk outside the building waiting for their respective pick-ups (Nell for her mother, DJ and Jay both kicking around until freshly-sixteen-year-old Nolan was finished with *his* day so he could drive the three of them home), they exchanged contact information.

Jay was pretty sure they'd found a friend who was going to stick. She'd learned to trust her instincts over things like that.

Nell clicked into their little carry over friend group from elementary school neatly. She had a talent for conversation. She didn't like silence, Jay learned quickly, but she didn't just fill it with noise for noise's sake - she was actually a really good listener, and would talk about whatever was on somebody's mind. She was always ready to listen to Leo talk about architecture or Jay ramble about literary devices or DJ gush about harmonies. And when nobody else had a topic, Nell could always find one.

Nell's cloud of white-blonde curls fell over clever blue eyes that sparkled with an intelligence she was always trying to play down and a grin that spoke of mischief even when it was perfectly, genuinely innocent. She got on with Jay like a house on fire.

She started hanging out with Jay and DJ and Leo and the twins on the regular - Dahlia and Liz had found their own group of friends a little separate from theirs, although both of them got along well enough with Nell, too. She even got along with Nolan.

One Saturday night in late November, DJ was sleeping over at Jay's house. That was nothing special, since they had sleepovers every few weeks and hung out after school every day. But DJ was sleeping over, and it was late. The sun had long since gone down, and the two fourteen-year-olds had already changed into their pajamas - Jay in an oversized t-shirt and gym shorts, DJ in the top from one set of PJs and the bottom from another - and brushed their teeth.

They were laying side-by-side in Jay's bed, both staring at the ceiling in the darkness.

"Hey, Jazzy?" DJ said softly. She sounded almost nervous. Jay wasn't really sure what to make of the nickname, either; it had been a while since DJ used it outside a sing-song *Jazzy-Jay*.

"Yeah, Deenie?" Jay replied, just as softly. She figured she might as well respond in kind to the nickname.

DJ let out a small, breathy laugh. "Can I tell you a secret?"

"You can always tell me secrets."

"You gotta promise you won't hate me."

Jay rolled onto her side to face DJ, concerned at the worry in her friend's voice. DJ's voice was mostly playful, but there was a genuine undercurrent of nerves there. It was too dark to really see DJ, she was more of a fuzzy grey smudge against the blackness in the room, but looking at that smudge felt *important*. "Dinah Elizabeth Jennings. I could *never* hate you. Ever."

DJ took a shaky breath. It sounded a little like a sob. DJ would be the first to say she was often overwhelmed, especially at fourteen, but this felt different. The worry in her voice was making Jay nervous.

"Deenie?" Jay said. She reached for DJ's hand, closing her fingers around DJ's between them. "Dinah, what's the matter?"

There was a long stretch of silence, where the only sound in the room was their breathing and all Jay could see of DJ was her moonlit outline but she couldn't tear her eyes away.

"I'm bisexual," DJ confessed finally, barely even a breath. "I like girls, Jazzy."

Oh.

"Oh," said Jay. A little bit of the tight anxiety in her chest at how stressed DJ seemed to be eased. "Oh, Deej, is that all?"

She reached across DJ, tugging her by the opposite shoulder until she rolled to face Jay, then collected her into her arms. That flickering flame lit back up in her chest, warming her to her fingertips as DJ burrowed her face into Jay's neck. Jay swallowed back the urge to say *me too*, because she didn't.

She wasn't.

Was she?

"It's okay, Deenie," Jay said instead. "I've got you, I've got you, and I'm not going anywhere, you hear me?"

"I hear you," DJ said. Jay ran her hand up and down DJ's back slowly, trying to soothe her.

"You didn't really think I'd hate you, did you, Dinah?" Jay asked softly.

She felt more than saw DJ shrug. "I don't know, I just - I realized and I - I don't know. I was just worried. That's the first time I've ever said it out loud."

"I could never, ever hate you," Jay said again. She shifted to rest her forehead against DJ's. It wasn't something she'd done often before, but the position felt familiar and grounding for Jay. She hoped it helped DJ feel the same way. "Do you think - I mean, do you want to tell people? Besides me, I mean."

"I don't know," said DJ. She sounded a little lost. "I just figured it out a few weeks ago, and I haven't said anything to anybody else. But keeping it a complete secret was kind of eating me up from the inside out, I had to tell you."

"Why me?" Jay blurted. "Why not Dolly?"

"I don't know," DJ said again. "You're my best friend. I knew you'd still love me no matter what. Not that Dolly wouldn't, but - I don't know. It felt - right. To tell you. Even though, like, I've spent all night trying to say it and I kind of felt like I was going to throw up right before and right after."

"Do you still feel like you're gonna be sick?"

"No." DJ laughs a little. "I feel fine. I feel good, actually."

"Good." Jay tipped her head back a little so she could press a small kiss to DJ's forehead. "I'm glad you feel good."

"Me too."

"I do love you, you know," Jay said. "You're my best friend, I think I love you more than Nolan. You're not getting rid of me that easy."

DJ laughs again. "I know. I love you, too, Jazzy-Jay."

"It's okay if you love me less than Dahlia though, since you're twins," Jay said, grinning. That warm, candle flame feeling in her chest is back at full force. DJ still sounded a little nervous, and Jay wanted to help her feel a little lighter before they went to sleep. "But since Nole is the worst you edge him out."

"Nole *is* kind of the worst," DJ said, still giggling. "He only offers you help on your math homework, like, once a week, and drives us to school, and -"

"Shut up, he ruined my perfect leaf pile the other day."

"Right, of course, that's definitely The Worst material, I should've known."

"You absolutely should've, you need to stay more on top of your Collins family news updates."

"If only my best friend in the world were capable of telling me about her day when her siblings cause her trouble."

"Yeah, if only."

They giggled over that for a while, and when DJ seemed like she'd finally fully calmed down, Jay rolled back onto her back. Jay's chest was still full of that flickering warmth that came with making DJ laugh.

"You ready to go to sleep, Deej?" she said quietly.

"Can I tell you one more secret first?" DJ replied, though she also rolled back to looking up at the ceiling.

"Sure. Anything, always."

DJ sighed, and Jay felt her bring her hands up, presumably to run them through her hair. "I've, uh, I've kinda got a crush on Nell. You can't tell anybody, okay?"

"Right, yeah, I won't. You gonna do anything about that?" Jay said. It came out automatically, a little hollow. She couldn't put her finger on exactly why, but there was this odd feeling in her chest at DJ's words. She still felt warm, but -

"I don't know if Nell even likes girls or anything," DJ said. "It's just a crush."

"Okay," said Jay. "Well, we can work with that."

- for the first time that Jay could remember, that warm, candle flame feeling in her chest? It didn't feel pleasant and comfortable and comforting. It felt too hot, it felt prickly and painful and uncomfortable under her skin all the way to her fingers.

For the first time in Jay's life, that little candle flame had turned into an inferno, and it felt like getting *burned*.

"Thanks, Jay," DJ said softly. "Goodnight."

"Night, Dee," Jay replied.

She stared up at the ceiling, her arms wrapped around her chest.

She didn't sleep well that night.

DJ decided in the morning that she wasn't quite ready to tell the rest of their friends that she wasn't straight.

"Even Nell?" Jay asked, ignoring the oddly hollow feeling in her chest as she said it.

DJ flushed bright red. "*Especially* Nell."

"Alright, alright, I hear you," said Jay. "You know I won't say anything. But our friends'll be good about it whenever you decide you're ready."

"I know," said DJ. She twisted the end of her hair around her fingertips. "Not yet, though. Hey, Jazzy-Jay, braid my hair?"

Jay nodded and shifted around so she was behind DJ and started combing through her hair with her fingertips to separate it into sections. She wasn't entirely sure what to make of how she was feeling about all of this, but at the very least she could keep moving forward like everything was normal. Braiding DJ's hair was easy and familiar and grounding, and it made it a little easier to pull herself back together. DJ didn't need to know that Jay was scrambled up inside.

So, yeah. Nothing really changed after that.

Only apparently sometime that fall someone had tattooed *Come out to me! I'll accept you!* across Jay's forehead, because about three weeks after DJ's midnight confession, Lizzie pulled Jay aside at school.

"Hey, Jay?" she said, shifting a little awkwardly on her feet. "I think I'm gay. Well, you know. Like, a lesbian."

"Cool," Jay blurted, because she wasn't really sure how else to respond. "Good for you, Liz."

Lizzie laughed, though. "Yeah."

"Uh, I'm glad you felt like you could tell me?" Jay said a little hesitantly.

"I knew you'd be cool about it," said Lizzie, smiling. "I'm trying to work myself up to telling everybody, you know? And I knew you'd - I don't know. You felt safe."

"Good," said Jay. "Good. I'm glad. Do you want a hug? This feels like a good time for a hug."

Lizzie laughed again. "Yeah, I'd like a hug. I think I need one."

Jay didn't need telling twice. She slipped her arms around Lizzie's waist and squeezed her tight. Lizzie hugged her back, her head resting against Jay's shoulder. They stayed like that for a long moment, and Jay could feel Lizzie's fingers running up and down the seam of her shirt sleeve. Jay held on as long as Lizzie needed her to, waiting until she felt her friend start to pull away before letting go.

"Thanks," Lizzie said.

"Any time," Jay said, then frowned. "That doesn't make sense."

"No, I get you," said Lizzie, laughing. "Thanks."

And then right after Christmas, Leo showed up at Jay's house. It was still winter break, and he appeared out of the blue in Jay's kitchen while she was baking and threw a mitten at her.

"Jay-Jay, can we talk?" he asked, but his tone made it feel more like a statement than a question. More like *We're going to talk now*.

Jay shrugged. "Yeah, sure. Meggie, don't eat all the cookies without me."

Meggie stuck her tongue out at her, which Jay took to mean that she wouldn't, but only because Nolan would stop her.

Jay led Leo out of the room, and the two of them made their way to Jay's room. She wasn't sure exactly what he wanted, but he seemed serious.

"What's up, bud?" she asked.

Leo picked at one of his fingernails for a moment. "I'm gay, Jay."

"I feel like I should be offended," Jay said, because an awkward *cool* wasn't going to cut it for Leo. "Was dating me really so bad it turned you off girls forever?"

Leo rolled his eyes. "I didn't know I was gay as an eighth grader!"

"It's only been like a year, Leo," Jay pointed out. "It's not like we're really that much older now."

"I feel older," said Leo. "I feel different."

"Yeah," said Jay. "I know what you mean."

She wasn't exactly sure *how* or *why* she felt different, really, but she did. Maybe it was something about being in high school, maybe it was about her birthday coming up, maybe it was just because some times you're more aware that you're growing up than others.

Leo nodded. "So, yeah. I'm gay. I didn't know before and now I do."

"Cool," Jay said, because she kind of couldn't help herself. "I'm, uh, happy for you?"

"You better be," said Leo. He threw his other mitten at her.

"You gonna tell the others?" Jay asked, raising an eyebrow.

"Eventually," Leo replied, shrugging. "I've gotta think about how. I just wanted to tell *you*."

"Thanks for - for trusting me."

Leo nodded.

It turned out that "eventually" was in the second week back at school, and his chosen method for making his announcement was to slam his hard-sided lunchbox down on the table and make all of their friends jump at the noise.

"I've got something I want to tell all of you!" Leo declared.

"Did you have to make me jump out of my skin to do it?" Dahlia asked, her eyes narrowed.

"Yes!" Leo said brightly. "Guys, this is important."

"Then get to it!" Mitchell said, tossing a goldfish at him. It sailed right past Leo's ear, missing him completely.

"*No* respect," said Leo. He rolled his eyes, then took a deep breath before saying, "I'm gay, guys."

The energy around the table changed in an instant. Not really in a negative way, just - the playful teasing stopped immediately, and everybody got serious. All eyes were firmly locked on Leo.

"Oh," said Mitchell.

Isaac hummed thoughtfully.

Lizzie popped up from her seat and held her hand out to Leo for a fist bump. "Same!"

"Thanks for telling us," DJ said. She smiled at him. "I'm proud of you, Leo. When we get to choir later, I'm going to sing you a song. A coming out song."

"What, not now?" Leo replied, laughing.

"I'm improvising it, you have to give me time," said DJ, grinning back at him. "And anyway, I don't have an instrument with me. You're waiting 'till I've got a piano."

"Well, thank you in advance for your musical support," said Leo.

(The song she made up did not rhyme, but it was remarkably catchy for the fact that she was making it up more or less on the spot.)

All of that was all well and good.

But the one that really caught Jay off guard was when Nell caught her after lunch one day in February.

"I have, like, the world's biggest crush on DJ," Nell said, her gaze a little dreamy. "You're, like, her best friend in the universe; do you think I've got a shot with her?"

"I'm sorry, did I miss the part of this year where you told us you're into girls?" Jay replied, trying to buy herself some time. She'd been sworn to secrecy about DJ's sexuality, after all, and she wasn't about to break DJ's confidence. But DJ *liked* Nell. So how to sidestep giving a straight answer without completely shutting Nell down?

"Oh," said Nell, laughing. "Uh, yeah. I'm into girls. Dunno about guys, really. But girls are - yeah. Like I said, DJ's -" she sighed. "She's something else, Jay. I could listen to her talk about chords for hours and hours, and those *eyes*?"

"Yeah, I get you," Jay said. There was something twisting in her stomach that she was pretty sure had nothing to do with the complicated balancing act she was trying to set up. "She's a catch."

She didn't need to hear Nell go on. She knew all about DJ's eyes.

(Oh, no.)

"So," Nell said, snapping Jay out of her head. "Do you think I've got a chance with her?"

Jay shifted on her feet, her hands in her pockets. Moments like this she wished her hair was still longer, because she found herself missing the ability to fiddle more subtly with the ends. She was still searching, desperately, for a non-answer that would be satisfying enough that Nell didn't just give up on the whole thing.

"I think you ought to ask DJ that," is what Jay settled on.

And Nell took her advice.

That afternoon, DJ ran up to Jay after last period. She threw her arms around Jay's neck, babbling excitedly about how Nell had asked her out in French class, how they had a *date* on Friday.

"She was really nervous," DJ told her while they walked to Nolan's car. "She said she wasn't sure if I'd be interested or anything but she had to ask. Can you believe it, Jazzy-Jay? Nellie *likes me!*"

"That's really great, Deej," Jay replied. She made herself smile at DJ, who beamed back at her with the kind of wide, bright smile that she usually saved for special occasions.

"What's great?" Nolan asked, raising an eyebrow.

"I've got a date on Friday!" DJ said excitedly, and then she launched into the whole thing again.

Jay took a few deep breaths. She wasn't sure why, but her chest felt almost tight. This was a good thing, this was great. DJ liked Nell a lot, and Nell liked DJ enough that she'd asked her out without being a hundred percent confident that she even liked girls.

Anything that made DJ this happy had to be a good thing.

So why did Jay feel like it had made all the air in the car disappear?

(Oh, *no.*)

"Can you come over to my house before?" DJ asked, squeezing Jay's hand. "To help me get ready and stuff? I feel like I'm going to, like, forget how to put an outfit together from nerves, and you know my style better than anybody. This is my first date *ever*, it's important. I need your help."

"Yeah," said Jay. That too-hot, flickery burning feeling in her chest was back. "Of course."

"You're the best, Jazz," DJ said. She squeezed her hand again.

Jay laughed, and it felt a little hollow but she was pretty sure it sounded mostly normal. "And don't you forget it, Deej."

DJ smiled at her, and it was that soft, easy smile that she only ever seemed to smile at Jay.

The burning feeling eased a little, into something closer to the warm, comfortable flame Jay was used to.

(Oh. *No*.)

Five: 10 Years Ago

Nell and DJ dated from midway through second semester of freshman year until early summer. Jay never found out exactly why they split up, and it didn't particularly matter.

At the end of the day, all Jay needed to know was that DJ showed up on her doorstep one afternoon in early June with her eyes red from crying and fell into Jay's arms as soon as she opened them for a hug.

The two of them spent a lot of time alone that summer. It's not that they didn't *want* to be with the others, it was just that their friend group happened to include Nell. And like Jay and Leo the previous year, it would be a surprise if Nell and DJ couldn't work things out and be friends again eventually, but for right now -

Well, for right now, DJ was hurting and so was Nell, and it was easier on the both of them (and everyone else who would've had to be around them) if they had a little space for a while. Jay happened to know, being in contact with the man himself, that Nell was spending a lot of time hanging out on her own with Leo while DJ was with Jay.

Yeah, that was definitely for the best for right now.

Jay and DJ spent a lot of time floating between their usual haunts from their childhood - the basement at the Collins house, their bedrooms, the treehouse in the Jenningses' back yard that they didn't quite fit into anymore but wedged themselves inside of anyway. It was a summer of long, lazy days spent sprawled in the grass in their yards and late nights lying awake at each other's houses long after the sun went down.

That was the first summer of nearly exclusively sundresses for Jay, and the first summer that DJ refused to wear a skirt even when a dress might've been more comfortable than what she'd picked. That was the summer of bare feet and journals carried everywhere, of soft music and tears.

DJ cried on and off a lot that summer, and Jay just sat with her until she was done, ready to comfort or distract depending on the day.

DJ was curled up on her bed, leaning into Jay under her arm. She wasn't crying now, just resting with her head on Jay's shoulder while Jay rubbed little circles on her back.

"I'm sorry," DJ said, hiccupping. "I know it's dumb to still be all worked up over this."

It was August.

"It's not dumb," said Jay. It wasn't dumb at all, really.

"It's just a high school romance," said DJ. "My first girlfriend. Everybody breaks up with their first girlfriend!" She sniffled. "I don't understand why I still feel so bad about it."

"Because," Jay said softly, "she was your first girlfriend. And you really liked her. That's allowed to suck, even if it happens to everybody."

DJ nodded. "It really does."

"Yeah, I know," said Jay, squeezing DJ tighter to her side. "I know, Dee, I know."

They sat like that for a while, the quiet of the early afternoon washing over them. David was at a friend's house and Dahlia was with Lizzie in the living room downstairs. Their parents were both at work.

DJ and Jay had the whole afternoon to themselves to help DJ sort herself out. School was approaching again quickly, and she was going to have to have *some* kind of handle on how she was feeling when they got back to having to see Nell all the time again.

"Can I play?" DJ asked, pulling away from Jay.

"Sure," said Jay, "go ahead. You know I'm never going to stop you, Deej."

DJ nodded, smiling. She crawled down to the foot of the bed, grabbing her guitar off of its stand and pulling it into her lap. She plucked the strings experimentally, checking the tuning.

Jay would never say so - she knew that double checking the tuning was as much a part of the grounding routine of playing as it was a practical step - but she would've been *very* surprised if it had fallen out of tune in the hour and a half at most since the last time DJ had played it.

Jay leaned back against the headboard, one knee pulled up to her chest. She loved watching DJ play. This summer had been a particular treat on that front, as DJ's favorite way to unwind and clear her head was playing and singing, and she'd spent a lot of time trying to work out new songs she was writing. As far as Jay knew, she was the only one who'd heard any of those experiments so far.

DJ had her hair down that day, falling in loose curls over her shoulders as she arranged the guitar in her lap. At this distance - just a few feet, just the length of the bed - Jay could just barely see those faint, faint freckles that dusted across the bridge of DJ's nose and just across the highest point of her cheeks. Her nails were painted green (by Jay a few days ago, on one of the few evenings this summer they'd sought out the company of Dahlia and Lizzie for a movie night), but it was chipped on her left hand at the tips.

Jay watched DJ's pale fingers move across the strings with practiced ease. DJ had only picked up guitar about two years or so ago, but it had come to her without too much struggle. She'd taken to flipping back and forth between this and piano depending on her mood, and Jay had spent many afternoons this summer curled in the corner of the Jenningses' living room couch, watching DJ's hands dance across the keys. She let her head fall back against the headboard, her eyes closing as DJ started singing.

She was singing one of the new ones she'd written in the last few months; it was still a little bit unpolished, but Jay adored it. There was something raw and sad in her voice as she sang it that made Jay's heart ache for her.

Actually, the singing probably wasn't the only reason for that.

Jay hadn't seen DJ really deeply upset very many times in the eleven years or so they'd known each other. DJ was a cautious person, and she rarely found herself in situations where she was likely to get hurt.

It broke Jay's heart to watch DJ's heart break, because DJ was her best friend in the universe. Because there was absolutely nothing at all that Jay could do to actually help save just being there. Being around. Listening, holding her. It didn't feel like enough, it never felt like enough.

The flickering warmth in Jay's chest that sometimes happened around DJ had been more *flickery* than Jay had ever known it this summer - warm and not burning anymore, but ebbing and flowing. It surged back with force any time she could draw a real chest laugh out of DJ, retreated almost to nothing when all she could do for DJ was sit there and wait for her to cry herself out.

DJ finished her song, but she didn't stop playing. She kept strumming, a little more aimlessly than before, drifting here and there in no particular pattern that Jay could discern.

"I'm sorry," DJ said, not for the first time. "For being such a wreck."

"Stop saying that," Jay replied, not for the first time.

"You've been so patient with me," said DJ. She kept strumming as they talked.

"That's my job," said Jay, shaking her head. "You're my best friend in the entire world, Deej. I'm here for you as long as you need somebody to listen."

"Thanks," DJ said, her voice a little distant. She chewed on her lower lip a little bit. "Do you think Nellie and I are going to be friends again? Like you and Leo?"

Jay hummed, thinking. "I think so. I hope so, you and Nell were good friends before. You've had some time, it might take a little more, but I think you can."

"I don't want this to ruin everything," said DJ. She switched to plucking out a melody - Jay recognised it as part of a song she'd just started working on a few days ago - her eyes on the strings and her own hands.

"Then it won't," Jay said, shrugging. "If you don't want that and Nellie doesn't, then you should be able to make being friends again work. I think you'd miss each other as friends if you didn't."

"You think Nellie would want that?" DJ said, looking up at Jay. She stopped playing.

Jay nodded. "Yeah, I do. Like I said, it might take you a little while, but I think you'll be okay in the long run."

DJ chewed on her lip for a moment, then nodded. "Okay."

Her hands started moving again, back to strumming now. That seemed to be the limit of DJ's ability to talk about this for now, because she started to hum one of her melodies again, though she didn't start fully singing again.

Jay stretched out, turning so that her head was on the bed looking up at DJ while she played, humming along in harmony.

There wasn't really that much that she could do to help DJ, besides just be here. Besides just making sure that DJ knew she wasn't alone and she had somebody with her who would listen.

But every ounce of what Jay *could* do, she was determined to do. Even if that was just singing along to a song here and there.

* * *

Sophomore year was the year that DJ really got into writing music. She had written a few songs before, obviously, like her silly coming out song and the one that had been the quiet theme to this summer, but it was like October hit and something clicked in DJ. Struck a chord, so to speak.

DJ and Nell were still giving each other a pretty wide berth, though they were starting to edge closer and closer to speaking again. DJ was still gravitating a little closer to Jay than usual when they were out with the group, while Nell clung a little closer to Leo.

They still spent a lot of time just the two of them.

During the school year that meant weaving more social time around actually doing homework and volleyball practice and games, but DJ was still working on new music with every free minute.

And Jay loved every minute of it.

DJ-writing-music was different to DJ-playing-music in energy; there was a focus in her that Jay hadn't really seen before. Not that DJ wasn't generally a focused person, or didn't focus on her music, but it didn't usually feel like this.

She always had a little notebook with her nowadays, for jotting down ideas. She carried it in her school bag and it was always nearby when they were at one of their houses.

(Jay had gifted it to her, near the start of the school year, after watching her scribble on any piece of paper that came to hand for most of the summer. It was small enough to fit into her back pocket most of the time, and she'd decorated the front cover with stickers of music notes and *DJ* written in block letters with a silver marker right in the center.)

Right now, they were in DJ's room. They'd spent more time at DJ's than Jay's lately, out of pure practicality - DJ could bring her guitar to Jay's, but not the piano.

Jay was on DJ's bed, having claimed it before they even got out of the car, theoretically working on her math homework. Theoretically being a key word here - she and geometry were having a hard time of it lately, and she was mostly just laying next to her math book and staring at the ceiling while DJ played guitar in a nest of pillows on the floor.

It was a very stop-and-start kind of playing, as DJ picked through a new idea.

"Are you stuck?" Jay said, rolling over and pushing up onto her elbows as DJ replayed the same phrase for the fourth time in a row.

"No," DJ said, playing it a fifth time. "Just thinking."

"About that chord progression?"

"Lyrics." DJ wrinkled her nose. "They're hard, Jazzy-Jay."

Jay laughed. "You're not even singing."

"I'm trying to *write* lyrics," said DJ. "Nothing's fitting the rhythm I want well."

"Take a break?" Jay suggested. "Work on something else for a bit. Or don't, and sing something you've already got worked out. Might make you feel better about it to remind yourself that you've figured this out before. I'm sure you'll get it to work again."

DJ smiled up at her, sweet and soft. The kind of smile that made that little candle flame light up in Jay's chest.

"That's a good idea," DJ said, and it had this teasing tone of reluctance that almost made Jay laugh out loud. "Have you got any requests?"

Jay hummed. "Whatever you want, Deej. Just one of yours, okay?"

"Yeah," said DJ. "One of mine."

She thought for a minute before starting to play. The song she settled on was familiar to Jay - very familiar, since it had been the one DJ kept circling back to all summer.

When she played it, it was soft and a little bit sad. Jay got the feeling it wouldn't always feel quite like this to hear, but right now - well, Jay was pretty sure this one was about Nell. She hadn't asked DJ about it, but the timing and the feel of it were right.

Jay let herself collapse onto her forearms, her chin resting on her wrists as she watched DJ play. Afternoons like this were nice.

Jay loved the company of their other friends, loved hanging out with their entire loud, chaotic group, but there was something really special about quiet days like this with just DJ. Something to do with the fact that DJ was her very best friend - though, arguably, not the oldest, since she'd met Isaac and DJ on the same day - and not at all to do with the warm flutter in her chest that always seemed to be there when she and DJ were close.

The last beams of late afternoon sunlight were coming in through the bedroom window, falling in little rectangular patches across the floor. DJ's voice drifted softly through the room, washing over Jay. She was warm and content - math homework notwithstanding - and enjoying the day. The blanket she was laying on was fuzzy and soft,

DJ's voice was calm and sweet, the day had been long and volleyball exhausting.

It was lovely.

Jay fell asleep.

She didn't really realize that was what was happening until she blinked awake a while later. The sunlight was gone, the dusty purple sky telling Jay that it wasn't full night yet but it was probably getting close.

When she woke up, DJ wasn't playing anymore. Instead, she was watching Jay with a hard-to-read expression on her face; that surprised Jay somewhat if only because she thought she knew how to read all of DJ's expressions.

She'd been reading them since they were five, after all. And maybe the difficulty was just because she was sleepy, but it still felt a little bit odd to be looking at DJ and not be able to guess at exactly what she was thinking or feeling.

"Oh, hey," DJ said, and the odd expression faded into a more familiar fond smile. "You're awake. Was I boring you?"

"Hmm?" said Jay. She stretched. "No, not at all. I love listening to you play."

"You fell asleep, Jazzy-Jay," said DJ. She sounded amused.

"Yeah, well," Jay said, "I'm comfortable. It was nice, you know, pretty singing and soft blankets and all."

"Are you awake now?" DJ said. "No more naps?"

"No more naps," Jay repeated.

"Good," said DJ. "Come down here and help me with this."

Intrigued, Jay slipped off of the bed to sit next to DJ on the floor in her nest of pillows. DJ still had her guitar on her lap, but it looked like she'd taken a break to work in her little notepad while Jay was asleep.

"You know the melody for Golden, right?" DJ asked.

"Of course," answered Jay, because how could she not after spending the whole summer listening to it.

"Can you sing it for me? With me, I mean? I want to try a harmony," said DJ.

Jay nodded and, once DJ started playing, started to sing and tried not to get too distracted when DJ joined in. Jay loved DJ's voice, and she always liked to hear new things DJ came up with.

Still, there was something awfully nice about singing *with* DJ, too, especially singing something DJ wrote.

The harmony was clearly still a work in progress - it mostly worked, their voices blending together in a satisfying way, but there were definitely still a few places where it was a little clashy in a non-intentional way.

When they finished, DJ wrinkled her nose.

"That wasn't great," said DJ.

"*Off*ense," said Jay, poking her side. "*I* did great."

"Yeah, Jazzy-Jay," DJ said with a laugh, "you did great. You should sing more often, actually, I'd forgotten how much I love your voice. But the harmony still needs work."

"Well, I'm happy to help," Jay replied, flushing faintly pink at the praise.

"Can we try it again?" DJ asked.

Jay nodded. "Sure."

So they did. They spent the rest of the evening on it - not just Golden, but a few others, too. All the way until Mrs. Jennings called them down for dinner, and then they ran back upstairs and flopped back into the pillows on the floor to keep singing together.

It was as close as Jay had ever come to collaborating with DJ on her music, since she didn't have any particular talent for playing herself. DJ had tried to teach her a little bit of guitar to mixed success - she had trouble with remembering the fingerings for chords, but when guided could work her way through without too much struggle - though there was no hope for her on piano - that was a mystery and a magic that Jay was content to leave to DJ, who'd been learning since they were five.

It was fun, and Jay could see how much lighter DJ seemed while she was writing and playing. If she could contribute to that, even a little bit, she was going to do it as much as she could. And if all she had to do was sing along, she thought as she watched DJ's face light up in a bright, easy grin, then she'd do that for the rest of her life.

Anything to make her best friend smile like that.

Six: 9 Years Ago

Jay and DJ had, by junior year, been playing volleyball for seven years. It was one of those things they started doing when they were kids and kind of just never stopped. They weren't on a club team or anything - just their high school team, which wasn't *super* good, but they had fun. Dahlia had played with them in middle school, but she wanted to do the musical in high school and the musical conflicted with the volleyball season.

DJ and Jay had a well established routine for game days - after school, Nolan drove them to Jay's house, they worked on their homework for a little while, and then they changed and did each other's hair before leaving for the game. The hair was a necessity for Jay, who in the three years or so since cutting hers to its current length had not yet mastered actually doing anything with it, at least not to a degree that would be secure enough for a high-energy volleyball game. It was more of a courtesy for DJ, who was more than capable of doing her own hair but preferred to let Jay do it.

It was late September, a game day. DJ was sitting criss-cross applesauce on the floor in front of the couch, quizzing Jay on French while she combed her fingers carefully through DJ's dark curls. She had half of DJ's hair swept to the side in a loose ponytail while she worked on braiding the other half.

"Um, *il a un* - shoot, no, don't help me," Jay said, pausing her braiding as she thought. "*Une baleine?*"

"*Un ballon,*" DJ corrected. "I'm pretty sure you said a whale."

"It's not my fault," Jay whined. "We spent, like, half of last year learning animals."

DJ snorted. "It was close, at least!"

"A *whale* is not close to a *balloon,* DJ," said Jay.

"It is in French!" DJ said, clearly trying to be comforting but landing somewhere entirely too close to amused.

Jay harrumphed and went back to braiding DJ's hair. She had never really mastered the art of the french braid on her own head, even when her hair was longer, but she'd had something like ten years of practice on DJ and Dahlia's. It came a lot easier when she could actually see what she was doing, and it didn't hurt her arms nearly as much.

Jay let herself sink into the repetition and familiarity of french braiding DJ's hair - over, over, pick up a new piece, over, pick up a new piece, over, repeat until the end of time - and let French *speaking* fall into background. She took care to make the braid tight and even, taking small sections of hair all the way to the nape of DJ's neck, then braiding tightly to the ends. There was no chance of these braids falling loose while they were playing. Once she'd tied off the first braid, she let down the loose ponytail on the other side before working her fingers through DJ's hair to mirror the braid on the second side.

After she tied off the second braid and admired her work for a moment, Jay patted DJ on the shoulders. "All done. Swap me?"

DJ nodded and got up from the floor. She stretched her legs for a moment before sitting down on the couch next to Jay and nudging her to move to the floor.

Jay did as she was asked, nestling in between DJ's long legs and resting her back against the back of the couch. Jay's bob was a little too short to do much with, definitely not the same full braids that DJ wore, but all they really needed to do was make sure it was securely out of her face.

DJ's fingernail dragged along the center of Jay's scalp, splitting her hair right down the middle. Unlike what Jay did with her hair, though, DJ also split Jay's hair across the crown of her head before tying one section out of the way, so that she had two rectangular sections from her hairline to the back of her head that DJ would braid, but the shorter hair at the back hung loose.

Jay had had her hair braided by DJ approximately a thousand times, so the sensations of her fingers moving through Jay's hair and the tension on her hair that followed in their wake was familiar, but even after all this time it was a soothing, grounding feeling. DJ was a meticulous braider - as well she needed to be to make sure that Jay's slippery hair would stay put where she wanted it - and her braids on Jay always turned out way neater than Jay's braids on her, though DJ insisted that she didn't mind.

She felt DJ tie off her first braid, tight to her scalp. She always french braided across the top of Jay's head and left a little pigtail at the end, since that was the most secure way to make sure Jay's hair wouldn't fall down halfway through the game. They'd learned from experience that braiding it all the way to the nape of her neck was a recipe for losing the strands around her ears, so it was better to just cut their losses and secure it as out of the way as possible. Jay always liked it because they still sort of matched like they always did when her hair was long, but she also got perky little pigtails that swung around in a satisfying way as a bonus.

Once she had her second hair tie in, they had to go change into their uniforms. They wore blue shirts with the St. Clare Chameleons logo on the front and their numbers on the back - DJ was number 12, and Jay was number 17 - with black shorts. They both had chunky knee pads on, too, though until they got to the court they tended to wear them around their ankles, since that made it easier to walk around when they weren't about to go diving for the floor.

DJ always looked *good* in her volleyball uniform. It was as much luck as anything else, Jay figured. She had the build for sports, especially this one. She was tall and lean, with long legs and arms. She'd looked gangly and stretched out for a few years, there, but at sixteen she was finally starting to grow into her height and in the athletic-fit clothes it really showed.

Jay, on the other hand - well, she had the muscle, she'd been playing sports just as long as DJ had, playing the *same* sports. But she was more compact, shorter and stockier. The cut of their uniform didn't flatter her the way it did DJ.

Not that she minded, really. No, really.

Jay knew that she was the less striking of the two of them at the best of times, since DJ was all soft curls and pretty blue eyes and long limbs, but on the volleyball court it was definitely multiplied by how well the uniform showed off her muscle. Jay was lucky enough to have probably the most beautiful best friend on the planet, and she was never going to complain a day about that. *And* she was a darn good outside hitter, too, so there was that.

They scarfed down some food before hopping back in the car and heading to school for the game - today's actually being played at St. Clare's, their first home game in a while - though Nolan didn't bother driving them back, tossing his keys to Jay instead.

It had to this point been a stunningly routine day - and, in fact, *remained* a stunningly routine day through about two-thirds of the evening.

And then DJ jumped for a block and landed wrong, even though she'd done it a thousand times before, and her ankle rolled underneath her.

A chill ran through Jay as DJ hit the floor, and she ran over - thankfully not far - sliding the last few feet to DJ's side on her knees.

"Deej!" she said, reaching for DJ.

She caught Jay's hand in hers, squeezing hard as she shifted into a more comfortable position. "Jay, it hurts."

"Yeah, Deej, I bet," Jay replied, trying to catch her own breath again.

DJ was remarkably calm about the whole thing, once she got over the initial bout of crying and swearing. Her ankle was starting to visibly swell up, and the coaches and referee were getting increasingly concerned. Once DJ was up to it, Jay and one of their other teammates helped her get back over to the bench.

Their coach was on the phone with 911, peppering DJ with questions as she got settled. Jay dug through her bag, tucked under the seat where DJ has gingerly propped her leg up. She took it upon herself to call DJ's parents - probably one of the other adults would do it eventually, whenever they realized that her parents hadn't come to the game, but she wanted to feel at least a little bit like she could actually help. And anyway, Jay had DJ's parents' phone numbers saved to her favorites.

Jay did her best not to hover too much while they waited for DJ's parents and the paramedics to arrive.

"We've got her, Jazz," Mr. Jennings said when they arrived, trying and failing (due to DJ's impeccable braiding) to ruffle Jay's hair.

"Of course, Mr. J," said Jay.

"Dee's lucky she's got a friend like you looking out for her," said Mr. Jennings. "We'll let you know what's going on when we know, okay, kiddo?"

Jay nodded, feeling a little numb.

"She'll be alright," Mr. Jennings said. He looks over to his wife and daughter, deep in conversation with a paramedic. "Why don't you see if your coach wants you to stick out the game? Looks like we're about to head out."

Jay nodded again, distant. She gave Mrs. Jennings a small wave, which was returned over DJ's head. As the Jenningses make their slow way out of the gym, DJ called over her shoulder, "I'll text you once we know if it's broken, Jazzy!"

"You better!" Jay called back.

The game was cancelled, forfeited after the loss of time and the fact that the Chameleons were all a bit shaken up. Jay gathered up her things and anything of DJ's that the Jenningses missed and headed, alone, for the car.

"You're home early," her mom said as she came in the door. She hadn't even pushed her kneepads back down her legs.

"Game got called early," Jay said listlessly. "Deej got hurt, her parents had to take her to the ER."

"Oh, honey," Mom said, "is she alright? Are you alright? I'm sure that was scary."

"It was," Jay replied, a little distantly. "She's okay, though. Mostly. Her ankle's messed up, the paramedics thought it might be broken."

"Well, I'm sure they'll take good care of her," Mom said, her tone soothing. "Her parents were there?"

"Not at the game," Jay said, shrugging. Their parents didn't make every game anymore, but neither of the girls really cared. "I called them while Coach was on the phone with 911."

"Good thinking," said Mom. "I'm sure she'll be just fine, sweetheart. Why don't you go up to your room and change?"

Jay nodded.

She was more than a little shaken. It had scared her to see DJ fall, and even though she'd been in better spirits by the time her parents arrived, Jay could tell she'd been in a lot of pain.

She flopped onto her bed, staring up at the ceiling, still fully dressed in her volleyball clothes. She hadn't even taken off her shoes.

A little while later, her phone buzzed. It was laying on the mattress next to her, and she could see the screen light up in her periphery.

Jay rolled onto her side. It was a text from DJ, with a photo.

The photo was a selfie of DJ sitting in a hospital room giving a thumbs up, and the text read *Not broken!!* Which made Jay let out a breath of relief she hadn't even been holding. Sure, DJ was still hurt, but less than Jay had initially feared and that was something.

That was enough for Jay to shake off her lingering worry, and she rolled out of bed and actually changed into pajamas. She texted DJ back, something playfully teasing to cover just how worried she'd been, and then threw herself back into bed for the night. It was still early, but Jay felt absolutely exhausted.

It turned out to just be a bad sprain, which Jay counted as something close to a miracle. DJ was supposed to stay off of it for a few weeks, so she was on crutches and she wasn't going to be playing volleyball any time soon.

That did *not* stop her from going with Jay to every game over the course of the month or so that she was out. Their routine was still mostly the same - she and Jay would pile into Nolan's car and head home after school, she'd help Jay do her hair and they'd work on their homework, and then they'd climb back into Nolan's car and head out to the game. The main difference now being that DJ was taking a seat in the crowd, watching and cheering from the front row at every game.

She also insisted on painting *GO JAY* on one cheek and *#17!!* on the other.

For every.

Single.

Game.

(It was sweet, it really was, but it also made Jay's cheeks burn with embarrassment and something else harder to identify every time.)

"You really don't have to do that," Jay said, not for the first time, watching DJ write careful letters on her cheeks in blue eyeliner. She didn't have any face paint, she'd said on the first day, but blue eyeliner she apparently just had on hand.

"If the football team gets adoring fans in face paint, I don't see why volleyball shouldn't," DJ said without stopping.

"The rest of the team will think you're picking favorites."

"Pssh." DJ rolled her eyes. "Everyone in our entire high school knows who my favorite player on the team is, you've been my best friend for like a million years." She reached over and booped Jay's nose with her finger. "So deal with it, Jazzy-Jay. I'm going to support everybody, but especially you."

"Well don't try pulling any stunts, if you're playing cheerleader," said Jay. "We can't afford to have you breaking your other leg, too."

DJ laughed, a full, genuine chest laugh. "I'll do my best, but no guarantees. You know how into the game I get sometimes. And it's not broken, anyway, it's a *sprain*."

"To-may-to, to-mah-to, Deenie," Jay said, rolling her eyes. "You messed it up too bad to use."

"Granted," said DJ. "Man, I can't wait to play again, though."

"Well, don't push it," Jay said with a frown. She was tense just at the *idea* of DJ getting back out onto the court. She ducked her head, suddenly unable to look at DJ anymore. "I don't want to see you get hurt again."

"Hey," DJ said, nudging Jay's shoulder, "hey, look at me." She waited until Jay met her gaze again, then she smiled. "I'm okay. It hurt but I'll be fine, alright? It's already been a couple of weeks, it's mostly healed already."

"I know," said Jay. "I know, I just - I don't -"

She faltered, staring at DJ.

It was hard to articulate exactly how she was feeling, especially when she was staring at DJ's face looking like *that*. Sure, her expression was open and earnest and sympathetic, with those clear blue eyes wide and a sweet smile on her lips, but she also had *GO JA* written on her cheek in metallic blue, not even finished because she'd stopped writing partway through. It was a distracting combination of sympathy and absurdity that Jay was having trouble sorting through.

"I don't like when you get hurt," Jay finished in a small voice. If possible, DJ's gaze softened even more, her smile going a little bit sad.

"I know," DJ said softly. "I know. I don't like when you get hurt, either. That's life though, isn't it? I mean, all told we've been pretty lucky; even that time you fell down the stairs last year you didn't break anything."

"Yeah," said Jay.

"I'm okay," DJ said again. "We've played this long without either of us getting hurt. It's not likely to happen again any time soon."

"Just don't rush it," Jay told her. "We want you back, but not at the risk you won't be healed yet."

"I know," DJ said, nodding. "I promise, I won't push it." She set her eyeliner pencil down and tugged Jay in by the shoulders for a hug. "I'm *okay*, Jazzy-Jay."

"Yeah, you better be," Jay said, aiming to lighten the tone of the conversation a little. Jay didn't need DJ to know how much the injury was stressing her out.

Jay herself rarely left the ground fully while they played - she was a setter, and she'd never really mastered the jump-set, so her feet tended to stay firmly planted on the ground - but DJ did just about every time they made a play. This was the first time she'd missed a landing like this, just pure bad luck, but the possibility was always there. In the weeks since DJ got hurt, Jay had thought about that… probably entirely too many times for her own good.

DJ hummed, frowning.

"Hey, sit," she said, gesturing for Jay to take a seat on the floor in front of her "I've still got to do your hair."

Never mind that her *GO JA* was still unfinished.

Jay sat down, her legs crossed. DJ combed through her hair a few times with her fingers, then dragged a fingernail through to separate the sections, just like always. Jay tried to focus on the familiarity of the sensation - DJ had done this a thousand times before, and she went through the process with practiced ease. It was soothing and grounding and if she closed her eyes, Jay could imagine that this was one of their normal game days, and they were working through their normal routine, not this odd half-normal they were living in right now.

When she'd tied off both of the pigtails, DJ pressed a kiss to the crown of Jay's head.

"There you go," she said, grinning as Jay turned around to look at her. "Shake it around, make sure it's tight enough?"

Jay knew that it was, because DJ had done this enough times that there was no guesswork left to do, but she did as she was told anyway.

"All good," Jay said, smiling up at DJ after she finished. "It always is. Now finish your dumb cheek words. Or better yet! Don't, and wipe it off before we leave!"

DJ snorted. "Nah, Jazzy-Jay, not gonna happen. Thanks for reminding me." She winked, and picked her eyeliner pencil back up.

Jay rolled her eyes, but she couldn't suppress a smile.

Seven: 8 Years Ago

Jay realized on a *nothing* afternoon. They were in DJ's bedroom, it was a Saturday.

Jay spent most of her Saturdays with DJ.

So, yeah, they were in DJ's bedroom. Jay was sprawled on the bed, having laid claim to it as soon as she and DJ got home from volleyball. Her backpack was at the foot, open and empty, and she was surrounded by notebooks and the entire contents of her pencil pouch. She had thrown herself into their current English class assignment - writing a poem from a fictional point of view. The idea was that it was not supposed to be something personal; they were meant to be putting themselves into the shoes of another person and writing a poem in that voice.

Jay usually liked writing, but she was extremely, extremely stuck. She was taking a bit of a brain break because of that, just laying on her side and scrolling aimlessly through her phone and listening to DJ.

DJ was *not* working on her English homework. Jay knew for a fact that DJ hadn't started the project yet, but DJ was nothing if not a procrastinator.

No, DJ wasn't working on her English assignment. But she *was* writing.

She had her guitar on her lap, and a notepad and pen next to her. She was plucking her way through a melody, and every few lines she would pause, jot something down, and then keep going. A few times, she had paused, frowned, and restarted the phrase a little bit differently.

"Does that one have words yet?" Jay asked, picking her head up when DJ stopped playing for a moment.

"Hmm?" DJ replied. "Oh, uh. No, not yet. You know me - I'm gonna put that off as long as possible. I like the *idea* of lyrics, but writing them -" she shuddered theatrically.

Jay laughed. "One of these days, I'll write some for you. Save you the bit you hate."

"You'd be my favorite person in the world," said DJ. She strummed a little, grinning up at Jay from her spot on the floor.

"I'm already your favorite person in the world. Remember, you told me last week that I'd finally edged out Dolly after the pizza incident?"

DJ snorted. "Right, of course, how could I forget?"

"I don't know, Deej, you said it," said Jay, laughing. "Hey, sing to me?"

"I'm *busy*," DJ replied with an eyeroll. "Don't you have better things to do than pester me?"

"Literally never in my entire life," Jay said. "C'mon, please?"

"Let me finish this first, and then I will, okay?" said DJ. "I promise."

"I'll hold you to that," Jay said. She rolled over and tried to refocus back on her poem. It was still pretty slow going, but she was making a little bit of progress, maybe. DJ went back to plucking her way through her new melody.

It was probably forty minutes later that DJ threw a crumpled ball of notebook paper at Jay. "Hey. Hey, Jazzy-Jay. What do you want me to sing?"

"Anything," Jay said, then she reconsidered. "Wait, no. Golden?"

"Golden it is," DJ said, and then she started to play.

Jay was pretty sure DJ wrote Golden about Nell, although DJ never really confirmed her suspicions. It was one of the first songs DJ had ever written, as far as Jay knew. It had always been her favorite. It reminded her of that quiet summer after freshman year, of sunny mornings spent in the grass in Jay's back yard and late, late nights in this very bedroom.

Jay remembered the first time DJ ever sang it for her. It was a Saturday afternoon a lot like this, and they had been curled up here in DJ's bed watching a movie on her laptop when she had sat up suddenly and told Jay there was something she wanted to show her. She had said Jay was the first person that she had ever played it for, and it lit up that candle flame feeling in Jay's chest.

"We'd be golden, we'd be golden," DJ sang. She looked up at Jay, a soft smile on her face, and that little flame lit up all over again.

Jay loved hearing DJ sing, she always had. DJ had a clear mezzo-soprano voice, and it was just about Jay's favorite thing in the world to listen to. Especially when she was singing along to her guitar or the piano downstairs. And when DJ sang for Jay, it always felt like Jay was the only person in the world.

The room was silent except for DJ's voice and her guitar and the occasional shift of the mattress as Jay squirmed a little closer to the edge to watch DJ better. The light streaming in the window was warm and bright, casting rectangular spotlights on the floor near DJ's feet.

DJ sat with one leg out and the other curled underneath her, her eyes drifting closed as she sang through the bridge. There was always something wistful in her voice when she sang Golden, and it made Jay's heart ache and that fiery feeling dance under her skin.

In this light, at this angle, Jay could see every faint freckle on DJ's face. She could see the flyaway curls that had escaped from DJ's braid. Jay sighed softly, sinking into the feeling of this moment.

She could live in an afternoon like this forever. The bed was comfortable, DJ's voice was beautiful, and *oh*, she was in love with DJ.

Wait.

"Follow me home, stay there forever, I'd make the space, we'd be golden," DJ sang, blissfully unaware of Jay's world tilting off of its axis.

She was in love with DJ.

How long had *that* been going on?

A lot longer than just today, Jay realized. A *lot* longer.

And Jay was suddenly overcome with the urge to blurt the whole thing out to DJ as soon as she finished singing, only that was a terrible, terrible idea. This wasn't, Jay knew instinctively, just some fleeting crush. This was Jay loving DJ - the sun rises in the east, water is wet, Jay is in love with DJ. It was a shockingly foundational fact of her being, it turned out.

It was *not* something she should just go saying willy-nilly to the most important person in her life. After all, this is DJ. Not that DJ would have an overly negative reaction even if she didn't feel the same way, Jay figured, but it could make things weird.

Or worse, DJ *could* feel the same way, and they could date and it could not work out in the long run and then - no. That wasn't happening, she wasn't doing that.

DJ finished the song, humming the last line of melody, and then looked up at Jay, grinning. "Satisfied, Jazzy-Jay?"

Jay's heart caught fire at that sweet smile, and it was honestly remarkable that she'd never made the connection between the flame under her skin and the wash of emotions that always came over her when she saw DJ smile.

"Yeah," Jay choked out.

DJ's eyebrows crinkled together. "Are you alright, Jazz?"

"What? Yeah, I'm fine," said Jay. "I just love that song. You know."

"I do," DJ said, smiling again. "You just look a little -"

"Hey, Deenie?" Jay said suddenly. "I'm bi."

"Oh," said DJ. "*Oh.* Okay, cool. Welcome to the club."

Jay laughed. "It is a bit of a club, isn't it?"

"I would honestly have been more surprised if you were straight, Jazzy-girl," DJ said, grinning. "You've got way too many queer friends for that."

"We were all friends before anybody came out," Jay pointed out.

"We flocked together subconsciously," DJ insisted. "It's a thing."

"You and I have been friends since we were *five*."

"Yeah, your little baby gay heart called out to mine and we've been friends ever since."

Jay snorted. "Sure, Deej. Whatever you say."

"This occasion calls for pizza, I think," DJ said. "What pizza toppings say 'coming out celebration' to you, Jay? I feel like it should be half-and-half something."

"We don't need to get a pizza," Jay replied, her cheeks going pink.

"We do," said DJ. "This is important and I love you and we're getting pizza. If it makes you feel better, I definitely wanted pizza anyway, and now we've got a really good excuse."

"Ah, I see, using my milestone as an excuse for pizza, I can respect that," Jay said, ignoring the flickering warmth in her chest at DJ's casual *I love you*. They had always been the kind of friends to throw that around - it's true, anyway, it's always been true. Jay just hadn't noticed the fact that it was true in more ways than she'd originally considered, at least on her part.

She rolled onto her back, staring up at the ceiling.

"Wait!" DJ said, throwing another crumpled ball of notebook paper at Jay. "I've got to sing you the coming out song!"

"You don't," said Jay, laughing. "You don't, I've heard it like thirty times -"

But DJ already had her guitar in her hands again, strumming along to the silly song she'd made up the day Leo announced he was gay to their lunch table. The main appeal of the coming out song was that it tended to lighten the tension of an otherwise stressful moment, and its non-rhyming lyrics consisted mainly of "I'm so proud of you, way to go" which is pretty nice. But it had an annoying tendency to get stuck in one's head, because while the lyrics were just this side of nonsense, the melody was catchy as heck.

The wide grin on DJ's face as she sang it set that little fire in Jay's chest alight again. She would never say so, of course, but Jay could probably live quite happily in this moment forever. She felt warm and content and loved and wherever things went from here, she knew with absolute certainty that she'd at least taken a step in the right direction.

When Jay handed in her poem for the point of view assignment, she didn't really think anything of it. Sure, she'd accidentally ended up pouring her heart and soul into it, but it wasn't a big deal. She could hide that in the anonymity of the poem supposedly not being written in her own voice, and anyway, the only one who was ever going to read it was Mr. Hudson.

Unfortunately, she had massively underestimated the degree to which the universe wanted to mess with her over this DJ thing. *Massively*.

She'd thought channeling her feelings into this project would be enough, would be able to help her keep it all to her stupid self. It had seemed like a safe way to express the feeling, now she'd finally put a name to that firelight warmth that DJ always seemed to cause in her, since *telling* DJ about it wasn't an option.

Maybe someday, she hoped. But not now.

But again, the universe was messing with her *hard*. Because a week after they'd handed in the assignment they came into Hudson's room and every desk had a printout of a poem on it.

Jay's poem.

Oh, for the love of God.

"Hey, Mr. H?" Jay said, walking quickly back to the front of the room. "What's, uh - what's going on?"

"Hudson, Jasmine," Hudson corrected pointlessly. "You embraced the alternate voice assignment completely, and your resulting poem is one of the strongest in the class because of it. And since your class is always *begging* to shake things up, I thought it would be fun to read one of your works today. Not for analysis, obviously, just to share some strong writing with your peers." He patted Jay on the shoulder. "It's a compliment, Jasmine."

"Right," Jay said, feeling more than a little bit sick. She couldn't exactly say *please, no, it's personal* - after all, *not* being personal was sort of the point. Hudson probably figured that wouldn't even be an issue, assuming Hudson had given two seconds of thought to how she might feel about it.

"There's no need to be nervous," Hudson said. "It'll be fun."

"Sure," Jay said mechanically. "Fun."

She sat down at her desk, right between DJ and Leo because of *course* she sits right between her two best friends in this class, with Nell two seats behind her.

The bell rang, and Hudson called the class to attention. "I have a special treat for you today - we'll be starting by reading one of your classmates' works. The printout on your desks is Jasmine Collins's point of view poem. Miss Collins took the opportunity to deeply explore a different voice to her own, writing as a boy who's fallen in love with his friend. Miss Collins, would you read?"

Jay resisted the urge to snort. When she'd handed it in, she'd just said that it was the point of view of a *person* who'd fallen in love with their friend, *a boy* was entirely Hudson's own assumption.

"Right, sure," Jay said. She cleared her throat, stalling. DJ gave her a little thumbs up, which did not, in fact, make her feel any better. "So, it's called 'Candlelight.'"

And then she started reading.

Or, well. Not really reading, because the wording of it was burned into her brain from the moment that she first thought of it, stretched out across DJ's bed while she sang to her. More like reciting.

"*I've never felt butterflies in my stomach / I've never felt my heart skip a beat,*" Jay said slowly. She paused, chewing on her lower lip. "*But I think I know what it feels like to be in love.*"

She closed her eyes, trying to pretend that she couldn't feel DJ's eyes on her.

"*Love feels like an open flame.*

She lit a fire in my chest when we were kids
   Small and persistent
   Like a trick candle on a birthday cake
   I just can't put it out.

And I know that feeling is love

I know it's love when she smiles at me

That little soft one she never gives anyone else

And I can feel it flickering in my heart

I know it's love when she touches me

When she holds my hand to show me something

When she pulls me into a hug

And it warms me all the way to my fingertips

I know it's love

because I watched her fall in love

With someone else.

And for the first time in my life

That flame in my chest left me feeling like I'd been burned.

Love feels like an open flame.

It's warm, it's bright.

It's comforting.

It's hot, it's blinding.

It's dangerous.

But I look at her and I can't help thinking

Maybe a few burns are worth it."

Jay finished and opened her eyes, and as she did she realized that she was gripping her paper maybe a little bit too tightly.

She set it down on the desk, smoothing over the creases. In her periphery, she could see DJ still watching her, but her gaze was a little unfocused and distant.

"Thank you, Miss Collins," Hudson said, and mercifully that was pretty much the end of it. They talked about her poem briefly, with Hudson pointing out a few things that caught his eye about the voice, but the class moved on fairly quickly after that.

"A *boy's* point of view," Leo said skeptically as they walked to their next class. "Tell me honestly, Jay, was that poem *supposed* to be super gay or am I just projecting?"

Jay snorted. "Yeah, no, it's super gay. Or, I don't know, I meant it to be ambiguous, but -"

"It's super gay," Leo finished, laughing.

Jay nodded. "Yeah."

"Deej, what'd you think of it?" Leo asked, leaning around Jay to look at her.

DJ, who'd seemed to be pretty deep in her own head, made a slightly startled noise. "Oh, I really liked it. I think it's one of your best, Jazz. Gross of Hudson to spring it on you like that, though."

Jay wrinkled her nose."Yeah. Like, a day's warning would've been nice. I could've prepared myself, or, like. Died or something."

"Hey," said DJ, nudging her, "at least it was this point of view thing and not one of your personals, right?"

"Yeah," Jay said, and it came out a little hollow. "Right."

Nell cornered her right after their shared last period class, which DJ wasn't in.

"Your poem," she said, her arms crossed. She blew impatiently at the flyway curls floating into her face.

"What about it?" Jay replied. She tucked her hands into her pockets, trying to look nonchalant.

"It's about DJ," Nell said matter-of-factly.

"What?" said Jay. "No! *Nooo*, what could - why would you - I mean. Me? Write about DJ? It's a love poem, Nellie! And it's not - it's not my voice."

"If that's not your voice then I'm straight,"said Nell. "Look, I'm not going to tell her. I'm *not*. But Jay. *Jazz*."

"Nell," Jay said quietly, warning. "It's not. It's not about her, okay. It - it *can't* be about her."

"What would be so bad about that, really?" Nell said, softening a little. "Deej is your best friend in the universe. Isn't that what everybody always *wants*? For the person they love to be their best friend?"

"It's not that simple," said Jay. She couldn't quite meet Nell's eye. "It's not."

Nell fixed her with a flat stare. "Explain it to me."

"She's my best friend," Jay said softly. She swept her hair over her ear on one side. "She's always been my best friend, ever since we were itty bitty. That's not a relationship I can risk by - by getting other feelings involved. Things are *good* how they are, Nell, and Dinah deserves better than -"

"Than what?" Nell prompted when Jay didn't continue. "Than the only person in the world who probably knows her better than her twin sister? Than someone who wants the best for her and has stuck with her through every up and down she's ever had?"

"Me," Jay finished.

"You know that you're the person I was talking about, right?"

"I know, I know." Jay said, her gaze somewhere around her own toes. "I just - I can't be reckless with DJ. I don't know, maybe I'll tell her someday, but we're *eighteen.* We're almost definitely going to different colleges, and we'll be apart and - and that's going to suck already, and I don't want to lose her friendship by trying to jump into something else that'll be harder to maintain while we're not together." She kicks at a broken tile. "And all that is assuming she even likes me back."

Nell squeezed her upper arm, and Jay looked up at her. "I'll be honest, Jazz, that's - that's a way better reason not to say something than I expected you to have."

Jay smiled despite herself. "Oh, yeah?"

"Yeah," said Nell. "You can count on me not to tell her, I just - well, I wanted you to know I'd noticed. There's a chance she did, too."

"I doubt it," said Jay, shaking her head. "She'd've said something."

Nell hummed, seeming unconvinced. "Maybe."

"But yeah, if I go for it with Deej -" Jay ran her fingers through her hair, dragging her nails across her scalp - "I've got to be in it for the long haul with her, if I go for it. And I can't do that now."

Nell nodded. "Your secret's safe with me."

"Thanks, Nellie," said Jay.

"Jazzy-Jay!" DJ called from down the hall, waving. "Hop to! David has a basketball game tonight and you know being on time for that is life-or-death!"

"I thought Davey's game was tomorrow!" Jay called back.

"Well you thought wrong!" said DJ. "Get moving, if we make good time we can finish our math and get dinner before the game!"

"I'm coming, I'm coming!"

Nell laughed. "You two are something else."

"Shut up," said Jay, shoving her lightly.

"For what it's worth, Jay-Jay, whenever you're ready to ask?" Nell said, her tone oddly sincere. "She'll say yes."

Jay's cheeks flushed, and despite her best effort to ignore it she felt the little fiery spark in her chest. "Yeah, yeah. If you say so."

And then she ran ahead to meet up with DJ, leaving the silently smirking Nell in her wake.

Eight: 7 Years Ago

Jay knew the exact moment when DJ spotted her, because she heard DJ's delighted squeal even before she'd found her friend in the crowd. DJ's advantage for being tall, she supposed. And the home-field advantage, too.

"Jazzy-Jay!" she called, waving. Jay finally spotted her, bounding toward her with her ponytail swinging wildly as she ran.

Jay, who'd been leaning against her car, perked up at the sound of DJ's voice, waved back. "Dinah-binah!"

DJ finally reached her, and she swept Jay into an enthusiastic hug, lifting her off of her feet and spinning her around a few times.

This was the longest the two of them had gone without seeing each other since that summer when they were twelve when Jay did a six week Girl Scout sleep away camp. Longer even than that, since it had been fully seven weeks since they moved to school for their freshman year of college.

Jay inhaled deeply, breathing in the familiar smell of DJ's shampoo and her favorite laundry detergent. Her fingers dug into DJ's back a little; she clung on tight. Jay had had friends move away before, had lived at home for the last year with Nolan already in college, had gone away to summer camps and on long trips.

She had never missed anyone as heartachingly deeply as she had missed DJ these last few weeks. She wasn't really prepared to deal with that - the realization she had last year still floated around the back of her mind from time to time, but she was mostly doing a good job of ignoring it. Being in the same place as DJ for the first time since they moved to school was making it a lot, a *lot*, harder to pretend that all of that wasn't happening. The warm, flickering candle flame feeling in her chest had flared right back up the instant her eyes fell on DJ.

DJ set her down on her feet, her hands slipping up Jay's arms to the back of her neck as she stepped back. "Your hair!"

"My hair," Jay replied, grinning.

"You finally cut it!" said DJ. She ran her fingers through the hair at the back of Jay's head, where there's been the most change. "It looks so good!"

"Thanks, Deej," said Jay. She was warm all the way to her fingertips now, despite the biting late October breeze. "It was a hard sell for my mom, but I finally won on the 'I'm eighteen now and you can't actually stop me' argument."

DJ laughed. "This suits you so much more than the bob, Jazzy-Jay."

"Thanks," Jay said again. She ran her hand through the front section, flipping her bangs to one side. "It's just how I wanted it, too. I'm really happy with it."

"I'm happy *for* you," said DJ. She smiled softly at Jay, and moved her hand down to squeeze Jay's shoulder before finally letting her arms drop to her side. "I think the first time you told me you wanted it short-short was when we were, like, six. This is a long time coming, and it looks freakin' amazing."

"No kidding," said Jay. "I'm still, like, getting used to it and stuff after having longer hair for so long but I like it. I love it."

"You look *so* good, Jazz," DJ said again. She grabbed Jay's hand. "Okay, c'mon. It's cold, let's go inside."

They walked together, hand in hand, up to DJ's dorm room. DJ only let go of Jay to open the door, then gestured toward her side of the room. Jay scurried into the room and hurled herself onto the bed, landing with enough force that she bounced a little on impact.

DJ laughed. "One of these days you're going to do that, and you're either going to miss or bounce all the way off the mattress, and you'll crack your head open. And I *will* call 911 for you, but I'm going to laugh really hard the whole time."

"No you won't," Jay replied confidently. "You always say that, but when I fell down the stairs in sophomore year you were so worried about me that you *cried*."

"I didn't cry," said DJ. She shut the door behind her and crossed the room a little more slowly, flopping onto the bed next to Jay. "I was just worried."

"To tears!"

"Lies," DJ said, shaking her head.

"Nope, you can't convince me," said Jay. She reached over to playfully punch DJ's shoulder. "You *loooove* me."

"Well, yeah," said DJ. She rolled her eyes, grinning over at Jay. "But as your best friend it is my God-given right to make fun of you when you do stupid things."

"And I respect that," Jay said. "I'm just saying that I don't believe you'd be able to let yourself do it if I were actually badly hurt."

DJ hummed. "No comment."

"No comment means yes!" Jay punched the air in triumph, laying back on the mattress so she was punching straight forward. "You only ever say that when I'm right!"

"That is *not* true," said DJ. It totally *was* true, though. DJ never liked to give in on things like this, always preferring to sidestep rather than admit that Jay was right. It was a dance they were both very familiar with, being at eighteen years old fully thirteen years into it.

It was sort of surreal, how easily they fell back into their established patterns like they'd never been apart. But they *had* been apart. Seven weeks.

Even though they talked nearly every day, Jay had felt DJ's absence like a missing limb. It was one thing to know that DJ was her favorite person, even to be quietly in love with her, but another thing entirely to face the prospect of not being able to turn to her left and tell DJ whatever was on her mind whenever she wanted. They had spent their entire childhoods attached at the hip, and Jay had spent the last seven weeks wondering over and over why they decided not to go to the same college.

"Hey," Jay said suddenly, watching DJ twist a curl around her fingers, "I've missed you."

"I've missed you, too," DJ said softly.

(It was because this was the best school for DJ's music, and Jay's school was the best for her writing, and they weren't even that far apart. It would all be worth it in the end, Jay knew, but getting there felt like walking over broken glass.)

They stared at each other for a long moment, not saying anything.

The moment broke - shattered completely - when the door banged open, thrown wide by what appeared to be a pair of legs attached to a giant plush turtle.

"Deej, I made a bad life choice," a voice said from behind the turtle, slightly muffled.

DJ snorted. "Was that bad life choice purchasing a three-foot-tall stuffed animal?"

"No," the voice said. The turtle was lowered, just enough that a heavily freckled face popped up over it. "The three-foot-tall stuffed animal was a pleasant side effect. Sheldon here was my winnings from a bet with Chuck Kelly. You know that Halloween carnival? He made me ride every single one of those death trap rides - oh! Jay's here!"

"Jay's here," Jay said, waving. She sat up, propping herself on her hands.

"I thought that was the weekend of the twentieth?"

"I have some interesting news for you, Han," DJ said with a laugh. "It's the weekend of the twentieth." She turned toward Jay, while her roommate spluttered in shock. "Jay, this is Hannah."

"I figured," said Jay, also laughing.

Hannah tossed Sheldon the three-foot-tall turtle plush onto her bed, crossing the room to shake Jay's hand. "It's nice to finally meet you, Jay. I've heard a *lot* about you."

DJ flushed a little bit pink. "All terrible, of course."

"Right, I wouldn't expect anything else," said Jay. She smiled at Hannah. "I've heard a lot about you, too. You're a history major, right?"

"You got it," said Hannah, with double finger guns aimed at Jay. "Creative writing, yeah?"

Jay nodded. "Here's hoping I'll be able to actually do something with it."

"I'll drink to that," Hannah replied, laughing.

"Deenie here won't have any trouble with hers, though," Jay said, leaning into DJ. She reached for DJ's hand, threading her fingers through her friend's. "She's going to be famous before we even graduate."

"Lies," DJ said, but it came out a little shaky and soft. "Lies. Stop trying to get my hopes up, Jazz. I'll be happy if I can get some decent accompanist jobs."

"You've *heard* her play, right?" Jay said to Hannah, pushing DJ aside a little bit and leaning forward.

Hannah nodded, laughing. "Of course."

"And she's freaking amazing, right?"

"Of course."

"*See?*" said Jay, turning back to DJ. "See! You're amazing and I'm not the only one who thinks so."

DJ laughed, shaking her head. "No, *no*, Jazz -"

"I'm sorry, I can't hear you over how right I am," Jay said loudly. "La la la la la -"

"Shut *up*," DJ laughed, shoving Jay to one side. "I know what you're doing, I can see right through you!"

"Oh?" said Jay, raising her eyebrows as high as she could. "And what am I doing?"

"This is a ploy to get me to play for you," DJ accused.

"That depends," said Jay. "Is it working?"

"Han doesn't want to hear me sing for you," said DJ.

"Oh, Han doesn't mind one bit," Hannah said, a teasing smile on her face. She sat down on the edge of her own bed. "Go on, Deej, I know you're dying to. You've been saying for weeks how much you were looking forward to playing that new song for Jay."

"You played a new song for someone *else* first?" Jay said, mock offended. She knew she didn't have a claim on hearing DJ's songs first, although the idea did sting just a little bit.

"She did *not*," said Hannah. "Refused point blank to play it while I was in the room, said I had to wait for you to visit to hear it."

Jay felt a familiar spark of warmth in her chest at that. "Really?"

DJ wasn't looking at her, her face flushed. "Really."

"Deej!" Jay said, wrapping an arm around her and shaking her side to side a little. "*Deej*, now you've got to play."

"Fine," said DJ, wriggling out of Jay's grip. "*Fine*."

She got up from the bed, moving over to the desk chair that had been pulled up to her little electric keyboard. She turned the keyboard on, stretching a little while she waited for it to wake up.

"Get on with it!" Jay teased.

DJ stuck her tongue out. "If you give me any more hassle I'm just going to get the coming out song stuck in your head."

"The coming out song?" Hannah repeated, sounding a little confused.

"She wrote this *dumb song* when we were *freshmen* to, like, congratulate our friend for being gay," Jay said with an eyeroll. "And it's super dumb and silly but it's the ear-wormiest ear worm she's ever written, I swear. It'll get stuck in my head for weeks at a time."

"Ah, I see," said Hannah. "Valid threat."

"Don't make me follow through, Han doesn't deserve that," DJ said.

Jay mimed zipping her lips shut, which made DJ roll her eyes.

"*Thank* you," said DJ. "I'm calling it *Dawn* right now."

And then she set her hands on the keyboard and started to play.

Jay had watched DJ play piano since they were kids, but it still honestly mesmerized her. It seemed almost like magic, the ease with which her hands floated across the keyboard. The guitar Jay could kind of wrap her head around, but piano was a pure mystery to her and she never got tired of watching DJ play.

(Not that she got tired of watching DJ play guitar, either.)

Jay shifted on DJ's bed so she was laying on her stomach, propped up on her elbows facing DJ while she sang. She knew Hannah was still here, but she sort of faded into the background.

Jay only had eyes for DJ - for the soft smile on her face as she sang, for the rogue curl that fell over her right eye, for the faint flush on her lightly freckled cheeks. The harsh, artificial lighting in this room did her no favors, and yet she still managed to take Jay's breath away.

DJ looked over at her, and those clear blue eyes met Jay's. Jay felt her breath catch.

"Living in the quiet -" DJ stumbled then, her fingers falling on a wrong chord and her voice dying for a moment. She tore her eyes away from Jay, flushing red. She went back a phrase or so and picked it up again. *"Living in the quiet before dawn."*

DJ didn't look at Jay again until she finished the song, but when she did she still didn't quite meet Jay's eye. "It still needs a little bit of work, but -"

"I love it," Jay said. She always said that.

"You always say that," said DJ.

"It's always true," Jay replied honestly.

Hannah let out a soft chuckle. "You two are cute. I see why DJ wanted to save that for you, Jay, you're clearly her number one fan."

"Since the first time she ever played for me," Jay said. It felt a little bit like a confession, though she wasn't entirely sure to what.

Hannah studied her, her expression thoughtful. Jay had the odd, uncomfortable feeling that whatever it was Jay just confessed to, Hannah had heard between her words.

"That's sweet," said Hannah. She stood up suddenly. "I'll leave you two to hang out, I promised Chuck I'd meet him at the library once I'd put Sheldon away."

"Okay, cool," DJ said. "Tell Chuck I say hi."

Hannah nodded. "Will do. Nice to meet you, Jay. I'm sure we'll be seeing each other."

"I'm sure we will," Jay agreed.

That visit ended entirely too soon, *entirely* too soon, and before Jay knew it she was driving back to her own college.

The nice thing, though, was that she and DJ didn't go to school *too* too far apart, and visits every few weeks were not out of the question. Not necessarily ideal from a paying-for-gas perspective, but more than manageable.

A tiny, pessimistic bit of Jay wondered when DJ would get tired of the back-and-forth. When they would give into the inevitable and start to drift apart. The idea made Jay's heart ache, but she couldn't help thinking it.

It was midwinter, and Jay was curled in the corner where DJ's headboard met the wall, wrapped up in every blanket DJ had.

DJ was laying lazily across the foot of the bed, working on something in a notebook.

She sat up suddenly, her eyes fixed intently on Jay. "I have something I want to talk to you about."

This is it, thought Jay. *She's done.*

"What's up?" Jay asked, and some of her anxiety must have come through in her voice, because DJ's eyes widened.

"Oh, God, that sounded terrible, didn't it?" DJ said. "It's nothing bad, Jazzy-Jay. I swear."

Jay gave that a weak laugh. "If you say so."

"I've got something for you," DJ told her. She flipped through her notebook and held it out open for Jay to take.

"What's this, Deej?"

"I wrote you a song." DJ ran her fingers through her hair. "I mean, technically I wrote you a melody."

Jay looked down at the open page. Sure enough, the words on it are familiar - on one side is the text of her "Candlelight" poem from English class last year, and the other column is that same text rearranged to flow like song lyrics. The only major change is from the third person (*she*) to the second (*you*). "This is mine?"

"I know it was for that point of view project," DJ said, rubbing the back of her neck nervously. "So it's not, like, supposed to be your own voice. But it's stuck so firmly in my brain, it sounds *so much* like you to me." *Whoops.* "I mean - I don't know, really, but 'Candlelight' spoke to me, I haven't been able to get it out of my head since you wrote it. So I wrote a melody for it. Is that okay?"

"More than okay," said Jay. "Deej, I - can you play it for me?"

She didn't know exactly what it was about "Candlelight" that spoke to DJ, but there was something almost dizzying about the idea of DJ singing lyrics based on a poem that was written about *her*. There was no way DJ *knew* - there was no way. But still, it was making it a little hard to think straight.

If she wasn't careful, Jay was going to go blurting her feelings out right here and now.

"Yeah," said DJ, sounding a little breathless. "Yeah, of course."

She reached for her guitar, pulling it up onto the bed with her. She plucked at the strings for a moment, making sure it was in tune, then started to play.

"*I don't get skipped heartbeats,*" DJ started, not quite meeting Jay's eye,

"I don't get butterflies. But I think I still know what love feels like."

Jay was entranced. She couldn't help but feel that candlelight feeling now - a flickering warmth radiating out from the somewhere near her heart that reached all the way to her toes.

DJ's eyes were closed as she sang, and when she did open them when she reached the bridge there was something distant about her gaze.

It focused, sharpening to a point and directed directly at Jay, as she finished the song. *"I think some burns are worth the candlelight."*

There was this electric moment of quiet when she finished.

"Deej," Jay breathed. "Dinah. That was - I love it. Thank you."

"I - yeah," said DJ. "I'm glad you - thanks."

Jay leaned over, pulling DJ's guitar out of her hands and setting it aside. Once she was sure it was in a safe spot, she gave DJ a tight hug.

When she sat back, she grinned at her friend. "I should write you lyrics more often."

"You should," DJ replied, smiling back. It was that soft, quiet smile that usually came on the end of bouts of laughter, the one she always seemed to save just for Jay. "You know how much I love your words."

"I know," said Jay. "You'll have to sing that for me again later."

"A thousand times," said DJ. "You really liked it?"

"I loved it."

"You always say that."

"It's always true."

So, yeah. Jay was less worried that DJ would get tired of her after that. They spent the rest of that visit brainstorming ideas for new songs, songs that Jay would write lyrics for and DJ would write the music for. And the next one, and the next one.

Jay went back to school with her mind full of melodies and harmonies and DJ, DJ, DJ.

She felt completely on fire, to her fingertips and the tips of her toes, under the skin of her scalp. She'd given up on pushing the feeling aside now - she loved DJ, and that feeling wasn't going away.

Jay found herself humming DJ's melody for Candlelight as she drove home. She always loved DJ's songs, but she had a sneaking feeling this one would be her new favorite.

Nine: Six Years ago

DJ had a new boyfriend. Jay hadn't met him yet, but she'd been hearing about him nearly constantly since he'd asked DJ out at the beginning of the semester. This was the longest she and DJ had gone in a while without making it out to visit each other; they'd managed around once a month for most of last year, which felt like enough that they didn't miss each other too badly but not so much that they distracted each other or they felt like they didn't have a chance for social lives in college.

And Jay did have a social life outside of DJ. For one, she was actually now in pretty frequent text contact with DJ's roommate from last year, Hannah, with whom she'd hit it off pretty much immediately. Hannah and DJ were living with each other again, so Jay was looking forward to visiting for a bonus reason now.

But on her own campus, Jay had a little group of friends she'd spent a lot of last year accumulating. Weirdly, among that group was Spencer Shipton, who'd been in Jay's class from kindergarten to third grade before moving away, still wearing the thickest glasses she'd ever seen but now six-foot-five and going by Spence.

Her other friends were mostly classmates - Benny from first year seminar, Madison from writing and rhetoric, Emma-Grace from algebra - plus a few friends that had come along with classmates like Benny's roommate Josh, and Emma-Grace's boyfriend Caleb.

She was out with them now, enjoying an enthusiastic debate between Benny (a fashion major) and Emma-Grace (a communications major) over which Disney Renaissance movie had the best style break from the studio's 'usual' style for 2D animation. Jay wasn't exactly sure how they'd gotten to that point; she'd been present for the entire conversation, but she still wasn't sure. They both kept pulling up screenshots from their movies as evidence, though Jay wasn't clear who was meant to be moderating this or how they were intending to declare a winner. Most of their friends were just watching from the sidelines, amused.

(They were emphatically split between the '97 and '98 releases, and Madison and Josh kept egging them on, throwing in their own arguments and generally causing chaos.)

Jay was distracted from the battle of the animated movies by a text from DJ.

> *Dinah-Binah: Are you still coming this weekend? I've finally got sunset worked out and I want to play it for you*

Sunset being, of course, DJ's latest song. Jay had written the lyrics for it, at DJ's insistence, though they'd collaborated on what those lyrics should be about.

She replied quickly.

* * *

Jay: Yeah, of course. I can't wait to hear it!

Jay grinned. She'd been looking forward to this one for a while, ever since DJ first told her about the idea for it. It was mostly about endings, although they'd never used the word end once in the lyrics, and Jay was really curious what it was going to end up sounding like.

"Hey, goofy grin over there," Josh said, tossing a crumpled napkin at Jay. "Who are you texting? Everybody you know is already here."

"You got a boyfriend you haven't told us about, Jay?" Spence teased.

"What?" said Jay, looking up from her phone. She shook her head. "No, I'm texting DJ. Spence, do you remember DJ?"

Spence laughed. "Oh, yeah. The two of you were like magnets, always stuck together. You got a girlfriend, then, Jazz?"

Jay felt her cheeks heat up as her phone buzzed with another message. "No, DJ's just a friend. She's seeing someone, anyway."

Dinah-Binah: Amazing! See you then! Love you!

Spence hummed, pinning Jay with a gaze that seemed to cut right through to her core. She wasn't sure how she felt about it, dropping her own eyes back to her phone to reply.

Jay: Love you!

Jay made the executive decision, then, to change the subject by throwing a wrench in Benny and Emma-Grace's debate and seeing where that went.

"Hey, guys!" Jay said mischievously. "I think you're sleeping on the real answer here - *Atlantis* and *Treasure Planet* are where it's *at*."

Sure enough, that sparked a whole new wave of argument - not just from Benny and Emma-Grace but the whole group.

She didn't meet his eye again, but Jay could still feel Spence's eyes on her.

That weekend was Jay's first visit to DJ since the semester started, fully a month and a half into the year. Too long, by Jay's clock. She liked her school and she liked her school friends, but she'd always be happiest in DJ's orbit.

She'd known that for a while, and it didn't seem likely to change anytime soon.

DJ was waiting for her, and greeted her with enthusiasm as soon as she parked her car.

She lifted Jay off of her feet in a hug, spinning her around a few times before setting her back on the ground. "Hey, Jazzy-Jay!"

"Hey, Dinah-binah!" Jay replied, laughing. She felt lighter than she had in weeks, that ever-present candle flame warmth lighting up as soon as she saw DJ.

It wasn't that she felt bad at school, just -

She felt better with DJ.

Completely aside from any sappy, mushy input from her heart on the romantic front, DJ was Jay's very best friend in the world, and she was always going to be happier around her. That was sort of how it went.

"How are things?" said Jay, as if they hadn't spent the last six weeks texting almost constantly. "I'm dying to hear this new song."

"I'm dying to play it for you," DJ replied. She had a soft smile on her face, and she pulled Jay into her side with an arm around her shoulders. She directed the two of them toward her dorm, home of (among other things) her guitar. "Things are good, my classes are alright and Han's doing well."

"How are things with your boy?" Jay asked. She snaked her arm around DJ's waist while they walked.

"Really good," DJ said, a warm blush spreading across her pale cheeks. "He's really sweet, I think you're going to like him."

"How's Han feel about him?" Jay asked. "She's got good sense, if she approves I probably will, too."

"She gets along with him pretty well," said DJ. She sounded just the tiniest bit genuinely nervous. "It's important to me that you do, too, Jazzy-Jay."

"I'm sure I will," Jay said. She leaned into DJ a little. "*You* do, don't you?"

"Of course?"

"Then I'm sure I will," repeated Jay. "You've got good taste, Deenie."

DJ smiled. "Thanks, Jazzy."

They made it up to DJ's room. DJ deposited Jay on the bed, where she immediately kicked off her shoes and snuggled into the blankets and pillows. There was one on the bed that was a similar chunky knit to Jay's favorite couch blanket from the Jennings house - it wasn't the exact same blanket but the same kind, and she wrapped it around her shoulders happily.

DJ grabbed her guitar and climbed onto the bed next to her, sitting with her legs crossed facing Jay.

"Okay, it ended up being a little more upbeat than we'd talked about," DJ said. "So you've got to just roll with that, okay? I think it works, but you can tell me honestly if you hate it."

"I'm sure I won't," Jay said, rolling her eyes. "I never do."

"You're allowed to hate them, Jazz!"

"Yeah, I know I'm *allowed*. But you're amazing and it's never going to happen!"

"Shut up, you don't know that."

"I do. Play, would you?"

DJ stuck her tongue out, but she did start playing then. The tempo *was* a little quicker than Jay had been expecting - when they'd talked about the sound of it, DJ had seemed pretty certain she wanted it to have a soft, wistful feel. That was the tone Jay had been thinking of when she wrote the lyrics, too.

"And in that golden firelight, even my darkest days seem bright," DJ sings, her eyes closed. *"Knowing when all is done and through, at least, I'll be home with you."*

But it worked.

A lot better than Jay would have thought.

She found, by the end of the song, that she'd leaned forward over her crossed legs, elbows on her knees and blanket falling away from her shoulders.

"Deej." She leaned a little further forward, tapping DJ's leg. *"Deej.* How do you do that?"

"Do what?" said DJ, her brow furrowed. "It was the same as -"

"Shut up," said Jay. "You know what I mean. It's really good! It's, like, so much better than I thought it was going to be!"

"What, did you think it was going to be bad?"

"No! Never! Deej, that's what I'm saying!"

DJ laughed. "Okay, okay, I gotcha."

The door opened.

"Hey, Deej, I found you something," Hannah's voice said as she came into the room. She was trailed by a tall guy with dark, wavy hair a little bit longer than Jay's, a square jaw, and a goofy, crooked smile. "He was wandering around by the library looking like a lost puppy, so I thought I ought to return him to you."

"Hey, Deenie-baby," he said, confirming Jay's suspicion that this was The Boy. "And you must be Jay!"

Jay disentangled herself from DJ's blankets and climbed off of the bed to shake his hand. "That I am."

"I'm Johnny," he told her. Jay knew this, because DJ had talked about him a *lot*. "I've heard an awful lot about you, it's nice to finally put a face to the name. Well, no, I guess I've seen photos, but - still. It's nice to meet the famous Jazzy-Jay." Johnny punctuated that with another smile. It was still crooked, pulling more to the right side than the left. He had one dimple.

"I've heard a lot about you, too," Jay replied.

"All terrible, I'm sure," Johnny said good-naturedly.

"I've yet to hear a fault, actually," said Jay, grinning up at him. God, he had to be almost a full foot taller than her. "All praise of your pretty eyes and fluffy hair."

"Really?" Johnny said, but this was directed over Jay's head to DJ, who was still on her bed and blushing violently red.

"Yes, really," said DJ, smiling but avoiding his gaze. "I happen to *like* you."

"Aw, Deenie-baby!" said Johnny. He swept into the room, past Jay, over to peck DJ on the cheek.

While he and DJ were distracted, Jay caught Hannah's eye and mouthed *Deenie-baby?*

Hannah snorted. *I know*, she mouthed back.

It was silly and a little childish, and reminded Jay inescapably of Beanie Babies, but DJ seemed to like it and from Johnny's tone it seemed to be coming from a place of genuine affection, so Jay had to accept it as at least somewhat sweet. She would definitely be making fun of it with Hannah later, but not until Johnny was safely out of earshot and all most definitely in good fun.

"What have you two been up to since Jay got here?" Johnny asked, seeming sincerely interested. Jay was liking this boy more by the minute. He seemed sweet, and anybody who could coax a smile like that out of DJ was in her good books for sure.

"Not much," said Jay. "DJ was playing her new song for me."

"Our new song," DJ corrected firmly.

"Oh, the sunset one?" Hannah asked, looking excited.

"Does this mean that Han and I finally get to hear it?" Johnny said. He kissed DJ's temple, then looked over at Jay. "She's been *very* secretive about it. Apparently new songs are for Jay's ears only."

Jay laughed. "Is that so, Deej?"

"It's only fair, if you helped me write it," said DJ. "It's still a little unpolished, anyway -"

"If *that* was unpolished, I'd love to hear it done," said Jay, rolling her eyes. "It was amazing."

"Also, I'd like to point out that she absolutely does this with songs Jay didn't collaborate on," Hannah said, suppressing a laugh. "For evidence, see all of last year."

"It's tradition!" DJ protested. "Since when did it become tease DJ time, huh?"

Hannah pretended to check her watch - she wasn't wearing one - and Johnny shrugged.

"Well, Jay just got here," Johnny said. "I'm pretty sure that was the official start time - Hannah?"

"Yep, that sounds about right," Hannah agreed. She grinned at Jay. "Care to weigh in, Jay?"

"It's been tease DJ time for me since the sixth grade," said Jay, "and before that it was tease Dinah time. It's my contractual obligation as your best friend."

DJ groaned loudly, flopping back onto her mattress. "I should've known better than to introduce you guys, this is going to be the worst."

"Aw, Deenie-baby, we do it with love," Johnny said fondly.

Jay didn't miss the brief moment where DJ's eyes went wide at that - fair, as it was early in the relationship yet to talk about love, even in a playful way - nor the fact that her own heart tripped over it a little.

She wasn't jealous. DJ was happy, and that was Jay's priority first and foremost, and even if that weren't the case (unimaginable as the case may be) Jay had no claim over DJ. She'd never said a word about her own feelings, and she intended for it to stay that way. She was genuinely happy that this was working out for DJ, and she really, truly hoped it continued to work out.

But for just a second -

Well, for just a second she watched a whole future spin out in front of her. One where Johnny stuck around for the long haul and maybe he and DJ got married one day, one where Jay stayed DJ's best friend but never anything more, where she was Auntie Jay to DJ's kids. Would she regret never saying anything?

Was it already too late?

Jay tamped down the uncertainty bubbling up in her throat. DJ was happy with Johnny. Maybe that would last, maybe it wouldn't, but as long as Johnny was good to her, Jay was behind him a hundred percent.

There was no point worrying about might-bes or might-have-beens.

"Hey, Deej, why don't you play Sunset for Johnny and Han?" Jay said, and it came out a little bit caught but mostly, blessedly, normal. Hannah gave her a funny look but didn't say anything. DJ and Johnny didn't seem to notice.

"Yeah, alright," said DJ. She sat back up, reaching for her guitar again. Johnny sat down next to her, and Jay joined Hannah on the edge of her bed.

She tried not to listen too closely to the words.

* * *

Johnny was sweet and kind and Jay liked him a lot, actually. He didn't mind that Jay and DJ had a tendency to fall into old patterns and old jokes when they were together, always game to listen to the drawn out story behind a joke or comment or, just as often, content to stay in the dark. He was an artist, Jay had learned, and his Christmas present for DJ -

"Sorry, Deenie-baby, should I call it a Chanukah present?"

"No, hon, it's fine. Jay calls them Christmas presents, too. Right, Jazzy?"

"Yeah, and *Deej* gives *me* Chanukah presents. Call it whatever feels right, bro."

"Winter holiday present."

"Sure."

- was a little portrait of her and Jay that he'd based on a candid photo he'd snapped on Jay's first visit. He gave it to her on the last day of the semester, when Jay was there to pick DJ up for their drive home.

"This is really sweet, Johnny," DJ said, a little breathless. "I love it."

In the painting, the two of them were hanging off of each other like they do - DJ's arm was around Jay's shoulders while Jay's was around DJ's waist, and DJ had her head thrown back in a laugh. Jay was looking at her, a wide smile on her face.

It *was* sweet. Jay had to appreciate that of all the moments for Johnny to paint for DJ, he'd chosen this one of the two of them. He knew how important their friendship was to DJ, and had made that the centerpiece of his gift to her rather than something to do with their (still relatively new) relationship.

Quite honestly, Jay was rooting for Johnny, at least a little bit.

"You really got my good side there, Johnny-boy," said Jay, leaning around DJ to get a better look.

"It wasn't hard," Johnny said with a laugh. "It's easy to make sure someone looks good in a portrait when they're as happy as you two make each other when you're together. I just had to capture that."

"Thank you, Johnny," DJ said, kissing him on the cheek. "This is, like, one of the most thoughtful things anybody's ever given me."

"I tried," Johnny said. "Like, a lot, actually. I'm really glad you like it."

"It's going on my wall," said DJ.

Johnny beamed. "High honor."

"You bet."

"Not to break up the moment," Jay said, "and I mean that, you two are cute as a pair of very tall buttons, but Deej, we really ought to be getting going."

"Right," said DJ. "Of course."

"Bye Deenie-baby," Johnny said, kissing her soundly. "See you in a few weeks."

"Bye, Johnny. I'll miss you!"

"I'll miss you, too, babe."

Jay's stomach did an awkward lurch as Johnny and DJ kissed one more time. She got into the car, not watching.

DJ got in on the passenger's side just a moment after her, and they drove off.

"Deenie-baby is cute," Jay says carefully, "but so, *so* silly, Deej. How don't you laugh every time?"

"It's sweet!" DJ said, but she was giggling. "Look, he wanted to have something to call me that nobody else used. That's what he came up with."

"That's very cute," said Jay. "You're honestly sickeningly sweet."

"I like him a lot, Jay," DJ said softly. "A *lot* a lot."

"Good," Jay said. "Good. I hope it works out. I hope it lasts, I mean. He seems like a good egg."

DJ was still holding the portrait he'd done in her lap, and she looked down at it, tracing watercolor-Jay's face with her fingertips. "Yeah. He really is."

Ten: Five Years Ago

Come the fall of junior year, DJ and Johnny were still going strong. Jay and DJ still spent at least one weekend a month visiting each other last year, and had spent the summer in each other's pockets like always. Johnny visited for a week in June and DJ had gone to stay with his family for a few days in early August. Now they were back in school, and DJ was delighted to be back in near-constant proximity to Johnny again.

She told Jay so at least three times within the first week. At least.

Jay hadn't really had much luck with love herself, though she tried a few times last year. She had a few actual dates, a few hookups. Nothing that lasted, but that was alright. She was mostly just looking for something casual for now anyway.

Well.

She had been.

> *Hannah Louis: Hey so feel free to shoot me down if I've got*
> *all this completely wrong*
> > *Hannah Louis: But I feel like we've got a nice thing*

> *going and I was wondering if the next time you're in town*
> *I could steal you from DJ for a date?*

Jay tapped her fingernails against her phone case, thinking. She was a little tentative about getting involved with Hannah - not from lack of interest in Hannah herself, mostly because they didn't live in the same city and it could be more trouble than it was worth. *But* Hannah wasn't wrong; they had a really fun dynamic, Jay loved talking to her and they played off of each other well when they were together. They spent a lot of last year elbow to elbow across the table from DJ and Johnny, teasing them endlessly for how sweet and sappy and in love they were.

And Hannah had that soft, floaty red hair that Jay could spot across a crowd even though she wasn't very tall because it was just that eye-catching. Her skin was sprayed with freckles, too, and her eyes were a clear, bright green - greener than Jay's, which pulled more to the muted, hazel end. Hannah's eyes were true green, and they could pierce right through Jay straight through to her heart.

Yeah, okay, Jay had been nursing a bit of a crush on Hannah for a while. What could it hurt, really, to give it a shot?

Jay: I'd like that a lot.

And that was how Jay started dating Hannah. They made a plan to go out for dinner the next time Jay visited DJ - the weekend after next - and then Jay called DJ.

"You'll never guess what I've just done."

"I have a sneaking suspicion," said DJ, "that it has to do with my roommate jumping up and down with excitement in our kitchen."

"Hmm," said Jay. "It might."

"She told me she was going to ask you out," DJ told her. It was a voice-only call, no video, but Jay could practically see the grin on DJ's face. She was imagining that self-satisfied smile she always got when she'd gotten a scheme to go her way. "I encouraged her; I've seen how you look at her, Jazzy-Jay, all starry-eyed."

(A small, small part of Jay couldn't help thinking *oh, so you notice how I look at **her**?*)

"Yeah, yeah," Jay replied. "Well, I'm abandoning you for dinner on Saturday next time I'm there, deal with it."

"You know, I think I'll live," said DJ. "I hope this goes well for you guys, Jazz. I think you two could be a really good fit."

"I hope so," Jay said honestly. "I really, really do."

The date did go well, to no small amount of relief for Jay. It would've been awfully awkward if it hadn't. They kept seeing each other, carving little bits of time out for each other when Jay visited DJ and Hannah even making a few trips of her own out to Jay's campus.

And then in February, Nolan got engaged.

Nolan had been seeing the same girl since his freshman year of college, and now they were seniors and making plans for the future. Jay had met the girlfriend - now fiancée - a few times over the last few years, and she liked her a lot. She seemed nice and she made Nolan smile and since Nolan could be a bit of grump that was often no small feat.

Their parents were hosting a big engagement party for Nolan and his fiancée, Allie, and Jay and DJ were making a special trip home for it. A few of their friends were coming home for it, too, which Jay was looking forward to.

She and DJ were also both bringing their respective significant others along with them. Obviously Johnny had met their families and friends over the summer, but this was Hannah's first introduction.

"It'll be fun," Jay said for approximately the thousandth time. "You *wanted* to come, remember?"

"Yeah, I did," said Hannah. She kissed Jay's cheek. "I do! I want to be here, I just - your friends - what if they hate me?"

"They're not going to hate you," DJ said. She was laying flat on Jay's bed, her legs propped against the wall. "Honestly, Han, you'll fit right in."

"They're nice," Johnny put in from his seat on the floor. "Just loud."

DJ snorted. "I think that's the understatement of the century, *just loud.*"

"It's chaotic when we're all together," Jay agreed, "but fun. Just chill, okay? It'll be good."

And it was - their friends latched onto Hannah immediately, she meshed easily into their conversations and Leo and Nell liked her enough that they stopped giving Jay sad looks behind DJ's back.

(That was a habit that had started *before* DJ started dating Johnny, but had increased a hundredfold afterward; Jay figured they were trying to come across as sympathetic but it mostly made things worse. Generally, she didn't give it much thought, it was just a fact of life and not one she needed to pay much active attention to. The sky was blue, water was wet, Jay Collins was in love with DJ Jennings. But it was background, it had to be, and Nell and Leo frowning concernedly at her when DJ wasn't looking just brought it to the surface when Jay was happiest leaving it lie.)

Hannah was talking with Nell now, animatedly caught in a discussion about what sounded like something to do with math, and Jay was halfway across the room, watching. She couldn't fight down a grin, it felt really good to see how easily her girlfriend fit in with her childhood friends.

"She seems sweet," Nolan's voice said, making Jay jump. She hadn't noticed him coming up next to her. But sure enough, there he was at her shoulder, watching Nell and Hannah talk across the room, too.

"She is," said Jay, once she found her voice again. "I like her a lot."

"Good," said Nolan.

"Congrats, again," Jay said. She turned to look at her brother. It was sort of funny, how things like this made her feel so aware of the passage of time - sometimes, time felt so slow, like the days were creeping by at a snail's pace. Right now, though, it felt like they'd been kids yesterday. But here Nolan was - taller than Jay by a few inches, broad shouldered and steady. He looked like a real live adult, and Jay wasn't sure when that happened. "I can't believe you're getting married."

"Neither can I," Nolan said, smiling. "It's, like, kind of wild. Kind of overwhelming. Not really the getting married part, but the - the graduating, the rest of our lives. I'm just glad to know Allie's going to be right there with me."

"That's so sappy," Jay teased. She elbowed him. "That's *so* sappy, oh my God."

"What about you, Jazzy?" Nolan said softly. "You think Hannah's it?"

"It's too new for that kind of talk," said Jay. She looked away from Nolan, fiddling with the hem of her skirt. "I - maybe. Someday."

"I always thought it would be Deenie for you," said Nolan. Jay's head snaps back up, her eyes meeting Nolan's.

"Nole," Jay said quietly. It was too much, too much. The soft, sincere way he'd said it. The nickname nobody else ever seemed to use anymore.

The fact that Jay had always kind of thought that, too.

"I mean it," Nolan replied. He shrugged. "I know it's not really fair to you to say it, with how she and Johnny are, but I really - you two have always been something else." He squeezed Jay's arm. "I guess what I'm trying to say is, I'm sorry."

"I like Hannah a lot," said Jay. It was a little to the left of a logical response, and she knew it. She didn't know what to say to the other thing.

"I know," said Nolan. He studied her, green eyes fixed on his little sister's face. "I can tell."

Jay swallowed, her own gaze drifting back across the room toward Hannah and Nell.

Hannah was looking back, and when their eyes met she lit up. Jay tried to match the brightness in her smile.

"She's - yeah. I like her a lot," Jay said. "It's easier for that to be enough when people don't - I mean, Leo and Nellie both -" She sighed, running her fingers through her hair. "I don't think about Deej that way. I can't, because it's just circling through the same thoughts over and over, and she and Johnny are probably the real thing and I - I just need to focus on what I *have* got, okay?"

"Right," said Nolan. "Of course. I'm sorry for bringing it up."

Jay sighed. "No, it's alright."

"I just mean -" Nolan sighed, tucking his hands into his pockets. "I'm happy. I'm really happy. And I want to see you happy, too. Whether that's with Hannah or DJ or someone else or just on your own."

"I *am* happy, Nole," said Jay. "I promise."

"Good," said Nolan.

So that was that, and Nolan was engaged and Jay was seeing Hannah and she was *happy*.

And then DJ showed up on Jay's doorstep on a Thursday afternoon, her eyes glassy with tears and her guitar in its case slung over her shoulder.

"We broke up," she said, and that was about the end of DJ's ability to speak in sentences, it seemed.

She'd brought her guitar, but she didn't play it that night; that night they spent curled up in Jay's room, wrapped in the heavy, chunky knit blanket that Mrs. Jennings had given her for her last birthday. Jay held DJ while she cried herself out, her shoulders shaking. Jay combed through DJ's hair with her fingers, the movement slow and careful, trying to soothe her as best she could.

Jay didn't ask why DJ and Johnny had broken up or what happened.

It didn't matter.

What mattered was that DJ was here, DJ was hurting, and Jay was going to hold her while she fell apart and then help her put herself back together.

The next night, she played.

There wasn't anything new in the line up - not yet - but Jay couldn't help but notice the handful of times that DJ circled back to Golden.

"Sing with me?" DJ asked, plucking halfheartedly at her guitar's strings.

"Of course," said Jay. She could never say no to DJ, not about this. Not now.

DJ stayed with her through the weekend, driving back to school Sunday afternoon. She and Jay texted, if possible, even more frequently in the following weeks. Jay checked up on her through Hannah, too, for a while.

Only Hannah - well.

About three weeks before finals, Hannah visited Jay at school, too.

"I don't think I can do this senior year," she said, shifting her weight side to side over her feet. "It's been really nice, dating you. I like you a lot, Jazz, but - well. I feel like we both always knew this wasn't a forever thing, didn't we?"

"Hannah," Jay said, not sure where she was planning to go from there. How do you respond to that?

It was true, but how do you *say* that?

"It's okay, Jay," said Hannah, smiling. "The distance was manageable this year, but we'll be busier next year. Extra visits probably won't be in the cards, yeah?"

Jay shrugged. "We could make it work."

"We could," said Hannah. "But it would be a lot. Better just to call it now, when we can still be friends, than to wait for it all to blow up in our faces, I figure."

"You're not wrong," Jay conceded. She shoved her hands into her sweatshirt pocket, pushing the fabric down at the center with the force of it.

"And anyway," Hannah said, "DJ's not seeing Johnny anymore."

"*Han -*"

"I know that you like me," said Hannah, holding up a hand to calm Jay. "I know. But it's not like her, is it?"

"I'm sorry," Jay said, and she knew Hannah would take it as confirmation.

And, well.

Hannah would be right, she supposed.

"You don't have to be," Hannah replied. "You can't control that kind of thing." She twisted the end of her braid around her fingertips. "I know you; I know you wouldn't have gotten involved with me if there weren't really *something* there, but - I mean, I don't blame you."

"I'm *sorry*," Jay repeated, and she meant it.

"I know."

"Still friends, though?" asked Jay.

Hannah nodded firmly. "Still friends."

"Good."

"Do you want me to leave?" Hannah asked tentatively. It was Friday night, and the plan had been for her to visit for the weekend. "I can. I thought it'd be best to get it out of the way right off the bat -"

"Han," Jay interrupted, "I'm not making you drive all the way back now. It's late. We can still hang out, yeah? As friends?"

Hannah nodded again, a little more tentative this time. "Yeah. Yeah, okay. Cool."

It was a quiet summer.

In a lot of ways, the summer after junior year reminded Jay of the summer after their freshman year of high school. She and DJ spent a lot of time alone - it wasn't that they didn't *want* to be with their other friends, or that they had a strong reason not to seek them out, this time.

They just didn't.

They spent hours and hours and hours holed up in DJ's room at her parents' house, at Jay's, in their back yards, in the basement, in the treehouse.

DJ played a lot of music that summer, and Jay wrote a lot, too. Jay wrote a lot always, and DJ played a lot always, and yet that summer felt like *more* on both accounts. On all accounts.

Jay spent the summer with candle flame dancing under her skin; every brush of hands and whispered word sparked the feeling that much more, but now more than ever she knew nothing could come of it.

She was watching DJ sort through the worst heartbreak yet of her life, and now was not the time. She was sure there would never be a time, quite honestly, despite the looks she was getting all over again from Nell and Leo and Nolan when he visited, and even, occasionally, Mitchell Garner.

It was a summer of routines, too.

Every morning, Jay would wake up and have breakfast, then head over to DJ's house. She'd wave hello to any Jenningses downstairs - usually Dahlia, sometimes David, rarely their parents who were usually both at work by the time Jay came over - and head upstairs to DJ's room, where she'd inevitably find her scribbling in her notebook or strumming thoughtfully on her guitar.

The two of them would spend the morning in DJ's room, working on songs together or working separately on stories or poems and songs in each other's space. They'd have lunch together, sometimes out with their friends, and then retire back to DJ's room or to the living room with the piano or Jay's house.

Some nights, they'd have sleepovers, like they did when they were kids.

"How are you holding up, really?" DJ asked on one of those nights. She was combing her fingers through Jay's hair, dragging her fingernails across her scalp like she always used to to separate out the sections for her braids. Jay's hair was too short to braid, now.

"I'm alright," Jay said, mostly honestly. She tilted her head to one side, giving DJ a new angle on her scalp. "Really, I am. Han and I were never as serious as you and Johnny were."

"That doesn't mean it doesn't smart," said DJ.

"No," Jay conceded. "But I'm - it's okay. I'm okay."

"You'd tell me if you weren't, Jazzy-Jay?"

"I tell you everything, Deenie-bean."

Everything except for that one thing, of course. Jay knew better than to tell DJ about that one.

DJ hummed, her fingertips skating across Jay's scalp in soothing patterns. "You've spent so much of the last few months taking care of me. I just want to make sure I can do the same for you."

"You take such good care of me, Deej," Jay said, ignoring pointedly the way her heart skipped as she said it, the flickering flames licking at the inside of her skin everywhere DJ was touching her. "The best."

"Good," DJ said thoughtfully. "You're my best friend, Jay, and I love you, and I just - I really want you to be happy."

"I know, Deej," said Jay. "I want that for you, too."

They fell asleep late, late that night, both curled up on their sides with arms pillowed under their heads and their faces just a few inches apart, whispering into the darkness until they drifted into sleep.

Jay woke up the next morning in DJ's arms, the two of them having rolled into each other in the night and clung on, feeling warm and content and happy and loved.

I could wake up like this every day of my life, she thought sleepily. She knew better than to say so out loud.

Eleven: Four Years Ago

It was Dahlia's idea, to start with.

They were home in late October - Jay didn't really remember why - and over the craft table at the Jennings house, Dahlia looked up at her sister and said, "Dinah, why don't you post your music online somewhere?"

And DJ said, "Sorry, what?"

"Your music," Dahlia repeated, shrugging. "You write songs constantly - you and Jay - but you never do anything with it. Haven't you ever thought about, like, going to an open mic night or starting a video sharing channel or something?"

"Oh," said DJ. She looked at Jay. "Jazz, do you think I should?"

Jay laughed. "You know I love your music, Deej. What do *you* want?"

"I'm sure nobody'd watch, if I made videos of my own songs."

"Don't be *dumb*, DJ," David said, not looking up from the costume he was working on. "People would love it. Mom's always dying to show you off but you've never recorded anything in a way she can."

"You really think so?" DJ replied uncertainly.

"Yes," Dahlia, David, and Jay said in near perfect unison.

DJ's eyes flicked from Jay to her sister and back again. "I - I'll think about it."

The project they were working on was their Halloween costumes for a local event. It was a group costume, and they were going as an old school 3D movie, since calling DJ, Dahlia, and David 3D was an old family joke. DJ's was an all-red outfit with the letter D on her shirt, Dahlia's was all-blue with a D on the shirt, and David was in purple with a D on his shirt and meant to stand between them, while Jay wore a T-shirt for a movie that came out in 3D when they were kids, leggings, a sweatshirt (her go-to movie theatre clothes) and a pair of blue-red 3D glasses.

Jay wasn't entirely sure how they'd gotten roped into attending this event, since neither she, DJ, nor Dahlia usually came home at this time of year, but she wasn't mad about finally going through with the 3D group costume that DJ and Dahlia had been talking about since pretty much twenty minutes after David was born.

At the party, Jay nudged DJ again. "For real, Deej, you should post your music somewhere. I'd help you, if you wanted?"

"I don't think I could do it without you," DJ said, and there was something odd in her voice that Jay couldn't quite place.

"Tell me the day and I'll be there," said Jay. "Or bring your guitar and we can set up at my place. Whatever you want, Deenie, I'm there."

DJ smiled, that soft quiet one that always made Jay's little candle flame reach her fingertips. "What would I do without you, Jazzy-Jay?"

Jay shrugged, grinning. "I don't know, probably just, like, die of loneliness?"

"Something like that," replied DJ, laughing.

Anyway, that was that, really. Decision made.

Jay wasn't exactly sure what it was that settled it for DJ; she didn't know why hearing from Dahlia and David that it was a good idea wasn't enough, or why hearing it from her *was*. She just knew that she loved DJ's music, and she was really, really excited that other people were going to get a chance to love it, too.

They made a plan that day for the next time DJ visited Jay to be the day they got everything worked out and set up to film a first video, as a test.

The day arrived sooner than Jay felt quite ready for it, and she could see in DJ's face that she was feeling the same way.

"Are you sure?" Jay asked gently, partway through setting her camera up. DJ was pacing up and down Jay's living room, looking a little bit like she was going to throw up.

And this all to *film* her singing. Nobody else was even going to see it yet.

"Hmm?" said DJ. She paused her pacing, looking over at Jay. "Yeah, I'm sure, I just - I've been playing for years but I never really, like, *perform* my own songs, you know? It's just stressful. I'm anxious. But there's not really - it's not really founded, you know? I've just got to do it." She smiled. "And anyway, you're here. What could go wrong?"

"I think plenty," Jay said, smiling back, "since I've never done this before, either. We'll figure it out together, though."

"I just mean that it's hard to really be worried about it when you're with me," said DJ, still smiling softly at Jay. "You're my lucky charm, Jazzy-Jay."

"Oh," said Jay, feeling a familiar warmth flood through her. "I see."

They set DJ up on a stool from Jay's kitchen, against a carefully arranged backdrop that consisted of the neatest Jay's living room bookshelf had ever looked, a houseplant that was moved specifically for this occasion, and a framed photo of Jay and DJ that hung on the wall next to the bookshelf. Jay's camera was on a tripod - purchased specifically for the occasion - and they were hoping for the best as far as sound went because they didn't want to commit to a nice microphone if this wasn't something they were going to keep doing.

DJ was wearing the ancient polymer clay music note necklace Jay had given her when they were kids, in all its clumsy, thumbprinted glory. It fit more like a choker now, but DJ had insisted on wearing it (for the occasion).

Jay tried to think of a good way to make DJ feel more comfortable doing this - yeah, it was weird, it was new, but there *had* to be a way to help her feel less stiff and stressed.

She hummed to herself as she set up the camera and made sure DJ was in frame. She hit the record button.

"Okay, Deej, go ahead," Jay prompted.

DJ nodded and started to play. They had settled on *Dawn* for this first one, one DJ was comfortable with and wasn't too recent, but wasn't too personal to lead off with.

It was…

Well, quite honestly it was the most awkward Jay had seen DJ with a guitar in her hands since they were twelve years old and she had played for the first time.

"Deenie?" Jay said softly, stopping the recording after the song was done. "I think we're going to need another take. That was a little -"

"Terrible, I know," said DJ, shaking her head. "I don't know why, I can't shake it."

Jay chewed on her lower lip for a moment. "I've got an idea."

She dragged the armchair a little closer, turning it around to face DJ from behind the camera. Then she went into her bedroom and snagged the heavy, chunky knit blanket from Mrs. Jennings off of her bed, wrapping it around her shoulders before flopping into the armchair.

"How's this, Deenie-bean?" Jay said, snuggling into the chair. "Does it feel like home?"

DJ laughed. "I think *you* look awfully comfortable, but don't really see how that's meant to help *me*."

"Sing to me," Jay said simply. She shrugged, the movement amplified by the heavy blanket. "I'm close enough to the camera that it won't be weird if you're looking toward me instead of it, and if you're looking at me you won't be focused on the new, weird thing. Just the familiar part, right? You've sung to me a thousand times."

"More," said DJ with a soft laugh. "Easily."

"Exactly," said Jay. "So sing to me, and forget about everybody else, okay?"

DJ nodded. "It's worth a shot."

Jay hit the record button again, and DJ started to play. The change was almost instantaneous, and it made Jay's breath catch in her throat. DJ was looking right at her, past the camera, and singing just like she always had, and yet -

DJ singing was always electric, there was always something *more* in her voice and her face and her playing that made Jay's skin buzz, but there was something different about it this time. An intentionality, a focus. It made that little candle flame in Jay's chest spark into a bonfire, dancing under her skin all the way to her toes.

"Better?" said DJ, after Jay turned off the camera the second time.

"Amazing," Jay said, and it came out a little breathless. "God, Deej, I'll never get tired of hearing you sing. Really."

DJ flushed pink, which was especially noticeable since the little color she picked up over the summer was fading back into her winter paleness. "I'll take your word, Jazz."

From there, it was a bit of a process to get the video onto Jay's laptop and edited - not expertly, by any means, since they were a writer and a musician and between the two of them the video and sound editing experience was less than zero - and uploaded to the profile that DJ had set up a few days ago. After a long discussion, they opted to use DJ's real name on the account, rather than her nickname, so the channel was called *Dinah Jennings Music* and the icon was a more-or-less recent photo of her at the piano at her parents' house.

They sent the link to Dahlia and David and their moms and their high school friends. DJ figured that would probably be about the limit of its range - just people they knew, people who had heard her before.

It wasn't apparent right away, not for a long time, actually, but DJ was *wrong*.

The first time that DJ played at a local open mic night was about a month after they uploaded the first video to her channel.

It wasn't the first time that DJ had performed in front of a crowd. She had piano recitals all through her childhood, not to mention performing in the musicals at their elementary school. That was different, though, because none of that had been *her* music. She was no stranger to playing her own music for people, either, but those people were usually people that DJ knew, and usually only a handful at a time.

This was a crowded cafe near her college campus, and there were maybe three total people in the crowd that she knew.

Jay, who had made a special trip over on a Thursday just to be there for DJ for this show, could tell that DJ was nervous. Not just nervous but climbing the walls nervous. Double checked the tuning on her guitar four times nervous. Kept getting up and walking around before sitting back down just to do it again three minutes later nervous.

Around the fourth or fifth repetition of the latter habit, Jay caught DJ's wrist. "It's okay, Deenie. You're okay."

"What if I suck?" DJ asked quietly. "This isn't like the videos, Jay, what if I'm terrible? We can't just scrap that take and do it again!"

"You won't suck," said Jay. She squeezed DJ's wrist, running her thumb soothingly across the soft skin on her inner arm. "You won't, you know how I know?"

"How?" DJ said. She sounded heartbreakingly uncertain.

"Because you're an amazing singer," Jay said sincerely, "and you're an amazing songwriter, and you can play these songs in your sleep. And I'm here, and Han, and you can focus on us. Screw everybody else, yeah? You're just singing to me and Han, it's no different than when you were rehearsing in your apartment a few hours ago."

DJ took a deep breath. "Right, right. Okay. I've got this."

"You've got this."

"Thank you, Jazzy," DJ said, her voice low. "It really means a lot to me that you're here. That you're helping me with all of this."

"Of course I am," said Jay, shaking her head. "I'm your best friend. What kind of a best friend would I be if I didn't help you get your music into the world? If I didn't help you get your head on straight when you're stressed? A bad one, I think."

DJ flashed a quick smile. She still seemed nervous, but this little pep talk seemed to have done the trick.

She was still a few performers away, but she didn't get up again.

When it *was* her turn, DJ shot Jay a nervous smile before she walked up to the front of the room.

Jay grinned back and shot her a thumbs up.

"Hey," DJ said into the mic, "I'm Dinah, and I'm going to sing a song called *Snowfall*."

Jay had heard Snowfall something like a hundred times - like Dawn, it was old enough that it came to DJ easily, comfortably, but wasn't too close to her heart to share so soon. It had an upbeat tempo and a catchy chorus; it was one of the ones that always seemed to float to the top of the list of songs that got stuck in Jay's head.

DJ wrote it when they were seniors in high school, and it reminded Jay of their childhood. It was *about* their childhood, though not in so many words, so that was fair, she supposed.

Jay was sitting next to Hannah at a table near the front of the room.

(It should be weirder to be around Hannah like this, Jay thought, but in the end the much weirder feeling was the awareness that Johnny - who had been a staple of their group for nearly two whole years - *wasn't* there.)

They were clearly visible from where DJ was standing to play, and DJ's eyes were locked on them.

More specifically, Jay couldn't help being aware DJ's eyes were locked on *her*. It was just like that day they'd filmed her first video for her music channel a few weeks ago. Like the only way DJ could get through this was by treating it like she was just singing for Jay.

She couldn't deny that it felt pretty good to know she was anchoring DJ like that.

Jay stared back, not just because DJ was the current performer but because, well -

Who'd be able to tear their eyes from *that*?

DJ had spent a not insignificant amount of time anxiously getting ready today before they came to the cafe, and it showed. Her curls fell gracefully over her shoulders, her makeup was subtle but absolutely perfect. She was wearing a green shirt with buttons down the front and a pattern of small birds printed all over it and a pair of black skinny jeans with the cuffs rolled up.

In short, she looked wholly and completely *DJ*, and she was absolutely stunning.

By the end of the song she was grinning for real, fully into the music and the moment, her nerves faded away.

Jay couldn't help grinning back at her, the little candle flame in her chest warming her through her core.

DJ fell into her seat again after her performance, to Jay's right.

"How was it?" she said, but her smile was wide and she seemed excited.

"Really, really good, Dinah-binah," Jay said honestly. "Absolutely amazing. I loved every second of it."

"Thank you," said DJ. "Thank you so, so much, Jazzy. Not just for the compliment," she grabbed Jay's hand on the table, "for pushing me to do this. I'd never have done something like this without you in my corner."

"Of course I'm in your corner," Jay told her. "You're my best friend. I love you."

"I love you," replied DJ. She threw her arms around Jay in a tight hug. "Thank you, Jazzy. For real."

Twelve: Three Years Ago

"You know what's *not fair*?" DJ asked when Jay arrived to help her pack for the move.

"What's not fair, Dinah?" Jay replied dutifully.

"You go all bronze and beautiful in the summer," DJ said, waving a hand across Jay. She was wearing a sundress that showed off her freshly tanned arms and shoulders. She had taken to studying outside in the last few weeks of the semester, so even though it was barely June she had a head start on her summer tan. "And your hair does that thing where it sun bleaches a little bit gold at the ends and it's *gorgeous*. And then there's me, red as a stinkin' lobster if I even *think* about the sun."

Jay smiled at her. They did this every summer, usually right after DJ's first sunburn of the year. "No, Deej, that's not fair at all."

"Not even a little!" said DJ, throwing her hands in the air. Her cheeks and forehead were stained red from, presumably, her first unfortunate encounter with the sun of the year. "Who gave you the monopoly on being pretty in the summer, Jazz?"

"Probably whoever gave you the monopoly the rest of the year," Jay replied, ignoring pretty successfully the fuzzy, warm feeling the onslaught of compliments was giving her. "You've got to leave some pretty for the rest of us, Deenie-bean."

"You're *so* pretty," DJ grumbled, "that's my *point.*"

Jay laughed. "Right, yeah. Of course."

"You don't get to stand there looking like that and say *right* in that tone, missy," said DJ.

Jay shook her head. "Whatever you say, Deej. You ready to get moving?"

"Yes!" said DJ, her expression brightening. "Yes, oh my god, I cannot *wait* to get moving."

DJ's graduation was a few days ago, and she and Jay were moving into an apartment together in their hometown. DJ had a job lined up teaching piano to little kids that she could do between filming videos for her channel and gigs at local venues, having been recommended for the job by the woman who had been *her* first piano teacher when they were children. Jay was going to be working at her favorite small bookshop, which left her plenty of time to help DJ out with her videos and write (and write, and write, and write).

Jay moved in two weeks ago, since her semester ended sooner than DJ's. Most of their furniture had been hers - she'd been living alone in a small apartment for the last two years, so her parents and Nolan had come and helped her move from the old place into the new one with her couch and chairs and kitchen things, while most of the furniture from DJ's apartment was either being given away or moving with

Hannah instead.

DJ's things were mostly already in boxes, or at least there were half-filled boxes strewn around the whole apartment. The activity for the night was getting as much of DJ's remaining stuff organized and packed as possible, in anticipation of packing up their cars in the morning and driving to their new place.

It was slow going, mostly because Jay and DJ could do nothing without getting distracted every few minutes by jokes and conversation.

"If you'd just wear sunblock," Jay said, not for the first time. She knew this was a conversation that would go just about nowhere - DJ had been fair her whole twenty-two years of life and had yet to master not getting sunburned as soon as the weather took a turn for the summery.

"I wear so much sunblock!" DJ protested. "So much, Jazzy-Jay."

They'd been having this conversation since they were about ten.

"Do you *reapply* your sunblock?" asked Jay, raising an eyebrow. "I swear, Dolly has the same coloring as you and she never gets as many burns as you do in the summer."

Jay had yet to make any inroads into helping DJ solve the problem.

"Dolly is *magic*."

"Dolly wears her sunscreen!"

"I wear sunscreen, Jazz!"

That fact wasn't likely to change.

"I call BS," Hannah called from her room. "I've literally never seen you put sunscreen on, Deej."

"My *moisturiser* has SPF, Han-*nah*," DJ called back. "Shows what you know!"

"Do you *put more sunscreen on later*?" Jay asked again. "Deej. *Deej*. Do you reapply?"

"Yeah, when I'm, like, out!"

"I don't have answers for you, then," said Jay.

"I'm cursed," DJ said, shrugging. She picked up a book, turning it over to read the back cover before putting it into a box. "Cursed, I tell you."

"Get a big floppy sunhat," Jay suggested. "Does that work with your aesthetic?"

DJ shrugged. "No. But if that's what it takes to not turn into a literal cinder every summer, I might have to invest in one anyway."

Jay laughed. "A literal cinder?"

"Burnt to a *crisp*, Jazzy," DJ said emphatically. "To ashes! And no sympathy at all from my best friend in the universe. Hannah!"

"What?" Hannah said, still tucked away in her room.

"You're promoted to best best friend!"

"Yeah, I'll believe that when I see proof."

"I'll make you a badge."

"By the time you're done with it, you'll have re-promoted Jay. I know where I stand."

"Never!" said DJ. "She's so mean to me, Han!"

Jay poked her with a throw pillow.

"She's being the worst," DJ insisted.

"Oh, no," Jay said, laughing. "No, never. I'm trying to help you solve your problem, DJ. Would someone who was the worst do that?"

DJ stuck her tongue out. "You don't have to laugh while you're doing it, Jazz."

"I laugh at you because I love you," Jay said, still grinning. "It comes from the heart."

"I love you too," said DJ. "But you're still kind of the worst."

"I don't know what you're talking about," said Jay. "I'm obviously the best. I came all the way here to help you move."

DJ looked down at the book she'd just picked up. "I suppose you're right. Hannah, you're demoted again!"

"Yeah, I know!"

Jay and DJ dissolved into giggles that carried them through the next twenty minutes of packing.

When it came to the end of the night, the couch was home to no less than four boxes, which left exactly zero room for Jay to sleep.

She was just starting to move the boxes, when DJ put a hand on her shoulder.

"Just share with me, Jazz," she said. "It'll be easier than moving all this, and then we won't have to pick these off the floor in the morning."

"Is that alright?" Jay said, tipping her head to one side.

DJ laughed. "I wouldn't have offered if it weren't."

"Yeah, okay," said Jay, "fair."

So they brush their teeth and change into pajamas - Jay in a tank top and pants, DJ in a St. Clare Chameleons t-shirt and gym shorts - and then crawl into DJ's bed side-by-side.

They weren't touching when they fell asleep, but Jay knew how this went. She'd shared beds with DJ before, and she knew they were going to wake up entangled. Both of them were cuddle bugs, and they had both always drawn comfort from being close together, so it was basically an inevitability that they would gravitate toward each other in the night.

So when she woke up half under DJ's weight, it wasn't a surprise. It wasn't even unfamiliar. It was almost painfully familiar, actually.

Soft, early morning sunlight was streaming in through DJ's bedroom window, barely dulled by the gauzy curtains they hadn't taken down yet. DJ's head was resting on the dip between Jay's chest and her shoulder, curls that had come loose from her braid in the night brushing against Jay's jaw. Her arm was wrapped tightly around Jay's waist, and Jay's, snaked under DJ's head, was loosely draped across DJ's shoulders. Jay was pretty sure DJ's other arm was pinned somewhere between them, while Jay's outside hand was resting over DJ's. One of DJ's legs was kicked over Jay's, wedged between hers with their ankles interlocked.

Jay tipped her head to the side, resting her cheek against the top of DJ's head. She had woken up like this before, but it never stopped making her heart skip beats. It was just so comfortable, so domestic, so *almost* exactly everything she could ever want.

God, if the thought *I could wake up like this every morning of my life* crossed her mind one more time she was going to die of it, though.

Days like this were almost enough to make her want to tell DJ how she felt. They made her heart ache with longing - for this to be her everyday, for these moments to be known and certain and unspecial, for DJ to love her back the way that Jay loved DJ. But at the same time, that longing came hand-in-hand with a fear she couldn't shake.

That DJ *didn't* love Jay the way Jay loved her. That she would think it was weird, that she would want to stop being the kind of close, share everything, do everything together friends that they had always been if she knew.

The idea of losing DJ over this was too much to bear, so Jay kept her mouth shut.

"What's the matter?" DJ said sleepily, tipping her head back and blinking slowly at Jay.

"Hmm?" said Jay. "Nothing's the matter. Go back to sleep, it's still early."

"You're frowning," said DJ, her brow furrowing. "It's too early for frowns, Jazzy-Jay."

Jay chuckled. "I'm just thinking, Dinah-binah."

"Think less," said DJ, her grip around Jay's waist tightening. "Snuggle more. I'm warm and comfy, you should be warm and comfy."

"I *am* warm and comfy," Jay said, smiling.

"Then there's no need for frowning," DJ said with sleepy certainty. "Go back to sleep."

And who was Jay to argue, really?

She shifted slightly, adjusting her hold on DJ so that her arm wouldn't fall asleep from the angle it was at, and closed her eyes, drifting off again to the warm, content feeling that came with being curled up in bed with her favorite person in the world.

There would be time to worry about the rest later. There would be months and years of living together to worry about that.

For now, she had DJ in her arms and a candle flame in her chest lighting up her life.

Over the first few months she and DJ lived together, Jay started to notice new patterns forming. Some of them were extensions of existing patterns of behavior between them, some of them were brand new. Jay found she didn't really mind either, both felt exciting and domestic and *right*.

Jay curled up on one side of their couch in the evening after work, her laptop open on her lap as she worked through planning out a story concept.

DJ had pulled her keyboard over in front of the armchair, and then stacked up a couple of extra pillows so she was sitting at the right height to play it, since their armchair was a little low. She was playing and singing quietly, but in the stop-and-start way that told Jay she was still composing whatever it was she was working on.

This was what a lot of their evenings had looked like since they moved in together. It was a quiet sort of companionship that came hand-in-hand with the eighteen year friendship that let them sit in comfortable near-silence together without *needing* to fill it with anything. They could just work side-by-side in the quiet and exist.

That wasn't to say that they *didn't* talk, just that they didn't need to. And since Jay was generally not one for silence, that was nothing to sneeze at.

"What are you working on, Deej?" Jay asked, frowning down at her laptop.

"*Settled*," DJ replied. "What, don't you recognize your own lyrics?"

"I'm not going to lie to you," said Jay, "I wasn't listening that closely."

DJ laughed. "And what about you, Jazzy-Jay? What are you working on?"

"Fairy tale," Jay said, still frowning. "I'm stuck." She looked up at DJ, her brow still furrowed. "The bat shouldn't talk, right?"

"No," said DJ, her hands still moving across the keyboard without apparent conscious thought. "You don't have any other talking animals, right? It would be weird if she talked."

"Right, that's what I thought," said Jay. She chewed on her lower lip for a moment before speaking again. "I just can't get through the confession scene without *some* outside push."

DJ hummed thoughtfully, still playing. "Well, the bat and the dog are both pretty smart, right? Even though they don't talk?"

Jay nodded.

"So use that," said DJ, shrugging. "Just nonverbally."

Jay tipped her head to one side. "That might work. Thanks."

They fell back into comfortable quiet - not silence, because DJ was still working through Settled, but not conversation.

A little while later, DJ tossed her sweater across the room at Jay. "Hey, I think I've got it. Listen to this version?"

Jay dutifully looked up at DJ, half-closing the top of her laptop to focus on the song.

DJ smiled at her, the soft one that always made Jay's heart catch fire. "Okay, here goes."

DJ had started working on Settled something like two days after they'd moved into this apartment, insisting that something about their new apartment had her inspired, but it had taken a few months for her to get from a loose concept to something actually resembling a song. It was quiet, not too fast, and sort of felt like these evenings they spent working side-by-side.

Which, Jay supposed, was probably the point of it.

"I like it," she said when it was over.

"What's wrong with it?" DJ asked, tipping her head to one side. In fairness, that *was* unusually lackluster as Jay's praise for her songs went. Anything short of *I loved that* is usually a sign something still needs work.

"The bridge is a little awkward still," Jay admitted, shrugging. "That's probably on me, though, because it was definitely a lyric problem, not a melody problem."

DJ smiled at her, clearly deeply amused. "You're so funny, Jazz. You could just say you don't like it."

"I do like it, though," Jay said honestly. "It's just not done yet, and we both know it."

DJ laughed, high and clear. "I suppose you're right."

So that was what their evenings looked like most days. Sometimes Jay worked a little later, sometimes DJ did, but mostly they had the evenings to themselves. Writing and music were interspersed with TV and video games and reading on either end of the couch with their legs entangled, always together.

One day a week was video day - usually Saturday, which they both had off from work. They'd get the camera set up and do a couple of takes of whatever song was next on the list. DJ did a mix of her own original songs and covers for her channel, which was starting to gain a bit of a following. Sometimes they would decorate her background to go with the song, or shoot at a specific time of day to get just the right lighting - they'd done the video for Sunset in one try as pinky-gold light streamed in through their living room window.

One corner of their living room was the designated 'studio' space for her videos, where they had a framed painting on the wall (the one Johnny had given DJ for Christmas/Chanukah/Generic Winter Holiday the first year they'd been dating) next to one of their bookshelves (the only one they had arranged with aesthetic in mind over book accessibility logic), and their camera setup and DJ's seat were almost always set up and ready to go. Jay's spot to watch from and man the camera was usually one of the armchairs, but that got dragged back and forth every week.

For the last few weeks, DJ had been trying to convince Jay to sing in a video with her.

"Just once, come on," DJ pleaded. "You know Snowfall sounds better with the harmony."

"Your viewers will be disappointed at the drop in standards," said Jay.

DJ laughed. "Are you kidding? Jazz, I love your voice. Everybody else will, too."

"That is a bold and definitely false statement," Jay replied, shaking her head.

"Come on, please?" said DJ. "We can do two versions, one as a duet and one just me, okay? And whichever turns out better we use?"

Which is how Jay ended up featuring semi-regularly on DJ's channel, instead of just behind the scenes like she was meant to be.

That - and the playful fight over whether or not Jay would do it - became a routine, too.

Other bits of their developing routine were less showy. Jay got up early in the mornings, earlier than DJ, because most days she started at the bookshop midmorning and she liked having time to fully wake up and get her brain going before she had to leave.

She took to making breakfast for the both of them. Sometimes that was just pouring cereal into two bowls and waiting for DJ to wake up, other times it was full spreads of eggs and bacon and toast and potatoes; sometimes it was just pancakes.

Pancakes became a frequent enough star of their breakfast table that they took to making up their own dry mix ahead of time, once every few weeks. They took turns doing it, usually one of them measuring out dry ingredients to put into their plastic tub while the other made dinner, bumping their hips and elbows against each other playfully as they moved around each other in the kitchen. That became part of their routine, too.

Jay never seemed to be able to get the timing right on the breakfast/ tea balance, almost always starting the kettle too late or too early, never quite managing to get them both done at the same time. DJ didn't seem to mind, though, and that became routine, too.

There were other things -

DJ did laundry once a week, and she always grabbed Jay's hamper.

Jay loaded the dishwasher whenever it needed running, but DJ always put the dishes away.

Every once in a while they would sit down on their couch side-by-side and watch a movie, sometimes one they loved when they were young, sometimes a new one they were looking forward to, always something they both agreed on.

They brushed their teeth next to each other most evenings in their shared bathroom, and on the days that they didn't, Jay inevitably wandered out of her bedroom an hour or so later to coax DJ away from whatever she was working on that was keeping her up, because Jay couldn't sleep if she knew DJ was stressing in the living room.

They fell into patterns easily, easier even than Jay had expected. She had always known that they would be a good fit as roommates - you can't be friends as long as they have without knowing the worst of someone, and that gave them a leg up on solving problems - but she hadn't known just how good a fit they were. DJ tucked herself into open spaces in Jay's life like she was always meant to fit there, which was sort of remarkable if only because after eighteen years it seemed unbelievable to realize that there were open spaces for DJ that she hadn't already filled. And yet here they were, curled up comfortably on either end of their couch, filling those spaces.

Sometimes it took Jay's breath away.

That candle flame feeling never really went away anymore. She was just always warm, always fuzzy and content in her core to be in her best friend's orbit like this. Sometimes it flared up more than others, like when she made DJ laugh or she won that sweet, soft smile that she never seemed to give to anybody else.

But it was always there, and that became part of Jay's routine, too.

Thirteen: Two Years Ago

Jay knew something was up as soon as she unlocked the apartment door.

For one, DJ was standing there, just, like, waiting for her. The camera tripod for DJ's videos had been moved, pointing toward the door. The apartment - at least the part Jay could see from the doorway - had been picked up.

"Hey, Deej, uh," Jay said, "what's going on?"

"I have a surprise for you," said DJ. Her hair and makeup are done, and she was wearing shorts and an open short sleeved button down shirt over a tucked in t-shirt - real clothes, in short. People clothes. Something she'd wear out of the house.

"And you're... filming my reaction?" said Jay.

DJ nodded. "Come all the way in?"

Jay did, kicking the door shut behind her and kicking off her shoes, dropping her bag next to them. "What are you up to, Dinah?"

Her full name honestly almost felt wrong in Jay's mouth, the shape of it unfamiliar after nearly twenty years of Deenie and DJ and Deej. It wasn't that Jay never used it, in fact the sing-song *Dinah-Binah* rolled off of her tongue at least once a week, but Dinah alone felt unfinished. But Dinah was the name DJ used along with her music, and Jay had a sneaking suspicion that this surprise was music related. At the very least, she was being filmed like it was.

DJ held out a little gift bag. It had stars and planets on it, and blue tissue paper sticking out the top.

"It's our anniversary."

"I'm sure we met earlier in the year than this," said Jay. She thought back across their early friendship. "Yeah, first day of kindergarten would've been early September, Deej."

"Yeah, I know," said DJ, rolling her eyes. "December fifth, though, Jazzy. You visited me at college in December of Freshman year and I sang to you. That was five years ago, Jazz! That means it's been five years since I first sang you Candlelight."

"Wait, really?" Jay replied, stunned. The time had flown, sure, but some of her shock was coming from the fact that this is a date DJ had committed to memory.

"You bet," DJ said with a grin. "And, like, that's the first time I put your words to music, so I definitely count Candlelight as the beginning of our songwriting partnership. This is a big day!"

Jay wasn't sure that Candlelight could really count as a collaboration, not the way their recent songs were, since they hadn't... you know, collaborated. At all. They had created two separate parts that came together into a song, but it wasn't really a team effort. Still, Jay wasn't about to contradict DJ over it. If DJ wanted to consider

Candlelight the start of their partnership, who was Jay to argue, really?

Jay laughed. "Yeah, I suppose so."

"Open your gift," DJ said, holding it out closer to Jay.

Jay took it, holding it from the bottom with one hand while she dug through the blue tissue paper in the bag with the other.

She pulled out something cylindrical and heavy.

A candle in a glass jar.

Jay snorted. "A candle, Deej?"

"A candle!" DJ agreed, looking quite pleased with herself.

"It's a little on the nose, don't you think?" said Jay.

"It's lavender," DJ said, unbothered. "Which I know is your favorite. I thought it'd be a nice gesture."

"It is," Jay admitted.

"There's one other thing," said DJ.

"In the bag?" Jay asked. She was pretty sure the bag was empty.

"No, as a surprise," DJ said with a laugh. "I want you to be in the video this week."

"Besides this?" Jay asked, raising an eyebrow and waving toward the camera. "What, did you want me to sing Candlelight with you?"

Because *that* was never going to happen.

"Not exactly," said DJ. Her cheeks flushed faintly pink, though Jay was sure she only noticed because she knew DJ's face very, very well. It was subtle. "I was going to set up like - like we do in the evenings? On the couch? And just sing to you, like I do. Just with you on camera instead of behind it. Like, just flip the whole thing ninety degrees."

She smiled at Jay and it was nervous, like she genuinely thought Jay was going to say no.

(Like she genuinely thought Jay was *capable* of saying no to her, especially over something this easy.)

"Sure," said Jay.

"Really?"

"Yeah. Just let me change first?"

"Of course. Go ahead, I'll get everything set up."

Jay, on impulse, handed DJ her snazzy new candle. "Here. Ambiance."

"You're a genius, Jasmine Collins," said DJ, grinning.

Jay laughed and went to her bedroom, shrugging off her clothes from work in favor of a light dress and an oversized cardigan. Its sleeves reached just past her fingertips when she let them hang freely, and it was warm and comfortable and soft. Home clothes, but home clothes Jay was willing to be on camera in.

She was about to head back into the living room, but paused. If they were doing this, they ought to do it right.

She grabbed her heavy, chunky knit blanket off of the bed, wrapping it around her shoulders like a cape.

When she got back into the living room, DJ had moved the camera so it was set up across the coffee table from their couch, Jay's new lavender candle lit on the table and the rest of the table cleared (Jay wondered idly where the piles of books and note paper that usually littered their coffee table had been stashed).

"You ready?" DJ asked.

Jay shrugged. "Yeah. I mean, you're the one doing the hard part. I just get to sit there and watch you play. That's not exactly a hardship, Deej."

DJ chuckled softly. "Yeah, okay, I suppose you're not wrong."

She was already sitting on the couch, in a nest of pillows with her guitar on her lap. She waved across at the other side of the couch, indicating for Jay to sit down.

Jay did, taking a moment to settle into the corner where the arm met the back of the couch. She shifted the blanket around her so that it was wrapped loosely around her shoulders but also swept over her legs, curled up next to her with one of her feet tucked just barely underneath her body. It was a comfortable position, a comfortable circumstance (save the odd unfamiliarity of the camera pointed toward the couch).

Once Jay was settled, DJ smiled softly at her and started to play.

Jay loved Candlelight. It felt a little strange to hear, even after all this time, even after she'd written other songs with DJ, if only because this one wasn't ever meant to be set to music, but she still loved it.

Candlelight was to this day one of her favorite poems that she had ever written, maybe top of the list. She'd written it in a flurry of inspiration that warm, quiet afternoon in DJ's room. The day she realized what the candle flame feeling in her chest meant. What it *was*.

She hadn't meant to write it, really. She'd meant to do the assignment for class, but suddenly she had a poem about DJ in her hands and an ache of longing in her chest and all she could do was lie about it. Might as well hand it in anyway, right? She couldn't have known their teacher would love it so much he'd make her read it to the class.

She couldn't have known DJ would love it so much that she'd set it to music.

And oh, *oh* did Jay love this song.

She couldn't quite explain it, not to Leo or Nell or Nolan or Dolly or Lizzie and absolutely definitely not to DJ.

Part of the not explaining it thing came from the fact that, in theory, nobody knew that the poem had been written from her own heart. In practice, Jay knew full well that Nell and Leo both knew, had both clocked her for it and what it meant the day she had been made to read it in class. They both were, generally, kind enough to Jay not to remind her of that fact. DJ certainly didn't seem to know, though, and Jay was not about to tell her.

She sat there, across the couch from DJ, watching her fingers dance across the strings and watching her face as she sang - her eyes were closed at the start of it, her brow ever so slightly furrowed, but now she was looking right back at Jay. Jay couldn't tear her eyes away, completely transfixed.

The thing about Candlelight, for Jay, was that somehow DJ managed to capture a little fragment of Jay's soul when she put it to music. Not just the words, though that was easily the most obvious part. There was a softness to the song, a wistfulness, a quiet heartache that still managed to feel warm and almost inviting, and it came through in the tempo and in the chords and in the melody and in DJ's voice every time she'd ever sung it.

She played it on piano for Jay once, a while ago, and it had seemed like she was maybe still figuring out how she wanted the accompaniment to sound. But on piano, it had felt so much sadder. It struck a chord so deep in Jay that she had actually gotten up and left the room, her chest aching and tears prickling at her eyes. Jay didn't know if DJ had ever fully sorted out the piano version; she'd never played it on piano for her again.

Jay hoped, distantly, that DJ hadn't thought that she had disliked that version, or that she'd left because she didn't want to hear it. The problem was that, for all that the guitar version held a piece of Jay's soul, the piano version had seemed to hold her entire heart.

She sighed, sinking further into the present moment.

DJ's voice washed over her, and Jay just let herself enjoy it. DJ was singing softly - not too softly for the microphone they'd bought for the channel's first anniversary to pick up, but really only just enough for that - and her fingers moved over the strings with practiced ease. Jay tipped her head to one side, resting it against the back cushion of the couch, breathing in the smell of her little candle on the table. If she stretched her foot out a little bit more it would reach DJ's, their toes just touching under the blanket.

She did, and DJ's eyes flicked up from the spot on Jay's shoulder she'd been staring distantly toward, meeting Jay's gaze. She smiled around the words as she sang.

It was easy to forget the camera, and the fact that this was such a departure from the usual feel of their videos. This felt like any other evening, the two of them sitting on the couch together while DJ played and Jay's little candle flame flared all the way to the tips of her fingers.

DJ didn't know the song was about her.

Jay wondered, sometimes, if DJ had someone else in mind when she sang it. There was a quiet wistfulness to her voice, a distance, that made Jay feel like she must. She *must*.

Jay wondered, sometimes, who it was.

A tiny, hopeful part of her wondered (hoped) if it might be her, but a much larger and more logical part of her said that DJ wasn't the type of person to just hold onto information like that. If it were Jay, DJ would've said something. If anything, it was probably Johnny. DJ hadn't had a serious relationship since him, but Jay happened to know that he'd had a steady girlfriend since two months into senior year.

The idea that there was someone out there who made DJ sound like that made Jay's heart ache almost as much as hearing the song - poem - that she wrote about the love of her life sung unknowingly by the love of her life did.

The song ended, and DJ gave Jay another soft, almost sad smile.

Jay smiled back, her heart absolutely on fire. "Thank you, Dinah."

"Happy anniversary," DJ said softly.

"Happy anniversary," Jay echoed.

DJ got up and turned the camera off, setting her guitar on its stand. "Thanks for humoring me, Jazzy."

"Yeah," said Jay, her voice feeling a little off. Not quite hoarse, but a little bit rough around the edges anyway. "Of course. Anytime."

The rest of that evening felt strange after that, out of time. Like they'd exhausted their usual evening routine on something so far off of normal but at the same time very nearly so that they couldn't go back to how the night would've normally flowed.

DJ actually sat down to read, still opposite Jay, who dug her laptop out of the stack of things DJ had moved off of the coffee table so they wouldn't be in her shot. Jay tried to write, her focus drifting in and out as she stared at her word processor. DJ tried to read, fidgeting every few minutes and shifting her legs around.

DJ's toes brushed up against Jay's, and she looked up. She wasn't surprised, she found, to find DJ already looking back.

"Hey," Jay said.

"Hey," DJ replied.

Jay closed her laptop and set it aside, back onto the table where it usually lived. She pushed her feet out against DJ's, so the tips of her toes were just touching DJ's ankles, her feet resting on top of DJ's.

"This was a big deal for you, wasn't it?" Jay asked. She didn't know why she said it, it wasn't really a conscious thought, but as soon as she did she knew it was true.

"Yeah," DJ said, and it came out more as a rush of air than an actual word. "I don't know, Jay, like. It just - I - all of this wouldn't exist without you."

"I don't know what you mean, Deej," said Jay.

DJ shook her head. "The channel, the videos. Hell, most of my music. It wouldn't exist without you."

"The channel was Dolly's idea," Jay pointed out, her brow furrowed. "And you wrote music before I started writing with you."

DJ chewed on her lip for a moment. Jay could tell she was thinking of how to phrase whatever it was she wanted to say, and Jay let her figure it out. She didn't need to press further; DJ would talk when she talked.

"It's just - Jay," she said, her gaze soft but her expression serious. "*Jay*. Jazz. I couldn't do this without you."

Oh, thought Jay.

"Oh," Jay said.

"Remember the first video we filmed?" DJ said, stretching her legs out fully. Her toes just brushed against Jay's thighs, feet bracketing either side of her. She pulled Jay's own feet into her lap. "It was such a mess, I was so awkward. And then you got that blanket you love so much and you snuggled up on our chair and you said *sing to me* and it was good." She chewed her lip again, thinking. "I could never do this without you here."

"Well, I'm here," Jay said, because how else was she supposed to respond to that? "And I'm not going anywhere, you're stuck with me."

DJ flashed a smile before falling back into a more thoughtful expression. "Yeah, I know. That's - I don't take that for granted, Jazzy. That's what I'm trying to say."

"That's what you're trying to say?" Jay echoed. She couldn't put her finger on exactly why, but the statement rang just a little bit false to Jay's ears.

"Yeah," DJ said firmly, punctuating with a nod. "Celebrating this felt important to me. I know you think it's silly - and don't pretend you don't, I know you - but I really do consider it the beginning of our partnership as songwriters, and that's maybe my favorite thing that's ever happened to me. And - and I know Candlelight is your favorite."

"It is," said Jay, and it felt a little bit like a confession. She was pretty sure DJ didn't hear it as one, though. "It means a lot to me."

"I know," DJ said softly. She tapped her fingers against the top of Jay's foot. "I finished the piano accompaniment for it last week."

"Last week?" Jay said, surprised. The first time she played it for Jay on piano was months ago.

"You cried, last time," DJ said, and it was not quite an answer. "If I play it for you, will you cry again?"

"I didn't know you knew," said Jay. "That I cried."

"You had that look," DJ told her. "I've known you for eighteen years, Jazz. I know what you look like when you're about to cry."

"Of course you do," said Jay. She tipped her head to one side. "If I say yes, will that stop you from playing it for me?"

"I don't want to make you sad," DJ said.

"I want to hear it," Jay decided.

DJ hummed. "If you're sure?"

Jay nodded silently.

DJ got up, moving over to her keyboard.

It's wild, because DJ sang this for her just an hour or two ago, because DJ had sung this for her a thousand times, but Jay's heart still stuttered over the first few words. The quiet, sad quality absent in the guitar version was still there from last time, though this version of the accompaniment *was* more polished than the last time she'd played it for her.

Jay felt that prickling in her eyes, but she didn't look away this time. She felt that ache in her chest, the candle flame licking at the inside of her skin, not quite burning but not quite comfortable either.

It's wild, but Jay couldn't help getting swept away in the emotion of it all over again.

"Jay?" DJ said softly when she finished, her fingers still resting lightly on the keys.

"Deej, I love it," Jay said. *I love you*, she didn't say. "Thank you."

"Thank *you*," said DJ. "Thanks for being here, thanks for listening, thanks for always having my back. Thank you for this song, and for all the ones that came after."

Jay got up, then, and she crossed the room to pull DJ to her feet. She wrapped her arms around DJ's waist, and DJ's slipped around Jay's shoulders, and they stood there silently holding each other for a long time.

"You're my best friend in the world," Jay said. "There's nowhere I'd rather be than with you."

"There's nowhere I'd rather be than with you," DJ echoed. She pressed a kiss to Jay's hair. "I'm so glad you're my friend, Jazzy."

Nothing changed, after that, but for the first time Jay started to feel like maybe it could.

Fourteen: Last Year

Leo Cruz was engaged.

He'd called Jay and DJ the day after it happened, showing off his shiny new ring in the video call.

"DJ!" he said, fixing them with a stern look. Or, presumably, fixing *DJ* with a stern look, but since he was small and on the screen it was hard to really differentiate.

"What?" said DJ.

"I swear to God, Dinah Jennings, if you come to my wedding in a dress, you're uninvited," Leo said. He had a look in his eye like he was almost actually serious, too.

"My mother won't like that, Leo," DJ said long-sufferingly.

"Screw your mother, Deej," Leo said. "Screw her. Honestly. I'm inviting all of my favorite people and I expect you to look *happy* in photos, damn it!"

DJ let out a startled laugh. "I'm serious! Do you know how much trouble she'd give me if I showed up to your *wedding* in a suit?"

"Not as much as I'd give you if you don't!" said Leo. "Dinah, I say this with love, but you looked so unbelievably uncomfortable at Nolan's wedding that I thought you were going to crawl out of your own skin."

"*Thank you*," said Jay, nudging DJ aside. "I've told her that, like, nine hundred times, but it always circles back to her mom."

"I'm *sorry* that I don't want to disappoint her -"

"She has a whole Dahlia right there who wears dresses of her own free will," Jay said.

"Jay-Jay's right, DJ," said Leo, nodding. "I swear to God, before Nole's wedding, I hadn't seen you in a dress since, what, your Bat Mitzvah?"

DJ shook her head. "It wasn't that long."

"She's right," Jay said, and DJ made a little sound of surprise that Jay was backing her up until she added, "her mom made her wear a dress to the party after my Confirmation. That was, what, eighteen months later?"

DJ shoved her.

Jay shoved DJ back.

"You both know very well that my mom enforces dresses for every major family event," said DJ, crossing her arms.

"And you look like you want to die *every time*," said Leo. "I want to see you happy in my wedding photos, Deej. My wedding album will be ruined if you're scowling in every single background shot you're in."

"I don't scowl."

"You scowl," Jay and Leo said in unison.

Jay laughed. "You'd look so good in a suit, Dinah-bean."

"You'd look *happy* in a suit," Leo added. "We all know you would."

"I'll think about it," was all DJ would say to that.

"I'm just saying," said Leo, "this is my wedding and not your mom's, and if you *don't* come dressed in something you're actually happy in, I will not let you in. Or, like, Nellie won't let you in."

"Heard," said DJ, rolling her eyes.

"I'm trusting your better half there to help you with this," Leo said, nodding vaguely toward (theoretically) Jay.

"*Better half?*" DJ echoed, offended. "Excuse me! I am absolutely the better half here."

Jay snorted. "That's what you take issue with?"

"It is," said DJ.

"Jay-Jay," Leo said, ignoring her, "make sure Deej finds something she's happy in, okay? We're not gonna be super fancy, so it doesn't actually have to be a suit, just. If I can see her calves I'll know something's wrong. It's not a shorts kind of wedding."

"Believe me, Leo, I'm on it," said Jay. "I promise."

They signed off of the call before too long after that, and Jay slumped against DJ on the couch. "Deej, can you believe Leo's getting married?"

"Kind of no," said DJ, leaning her own weight back onto Jay. "It still sort of feels like yesterday we were ten years old."

"I was *Jasmine* then still," Jay said. "*Dee-nuh.*"

DJ laughed. "You're funny, Jazz."

"You still wore dresses then," said Jay, picking up the thread of the conversation they'd been having with Leo.

"Jay -"

"No, Deej, seriously," Jay said. "I'm trying to - I'm thinking about how much we've grown up since then, since we met him, you know? We're so much more *us* than we were when we were ten years old. You should embrace that."

"I do embrace that," said DJ, gesturing across her current outfit. It involved *suspenders*, because of course it did. "But there's embracing my sense of style and there's disappointing my mother's."

"Nole's wedding was different," said Jay, chewing the inside of her lip between thoughts. "Nole's wedding was different. That's family. If and when Dolly or Davey gets married, then your mom's got some room to push you around, I guess. But, like, your mom isn't even *going* to Leo's wedding."

"I guess," said DJ.

Jay was pretty sure that they could swing Mrs. Jennings on this, and even if they couldn't that it wouldn't really matter in the long run. At the end of the day, it's Leo's wedding and Leo wanted DJ to look and feel like herself, and that would have to be enough for DJ.

Jay chuckled. "It's funny, I think about it sometimes, like. Your mom with the dresses, mine with the hair. They just don't quite see *us*, do they? Just the little kids we were back then. When I was Jasmine, and you were Dinah."

"That's a funny way of thinking about it, Jazz," DJ replied, her brow faintly furrowed. "When you were Jasmine and I was Dinah. We still are."

"Deej," Jay said pointedly. "We've both gone almost exclusively by nicknames since, like, the sixth grade."

"I guess it isn't entirely unfair to delineate between our young childhood and now with our nicknames," DJ concedes. "It's just that I've never really thought of it like that."

"Thank you," said Jay. "Anyway all of that is to say that, like, you're not the person you were when you were a little kid and you should get to be the person you are *now* at our friend's wedding."

DJ hummed. "I'll take it under consideration, is that enough for you?"

"I'll take it, but only because that means I'm going to win," Jay said, grinning. "I love the person you've grown into. And anyway, you look so good all dressed up. You should share that with the world." She winked at her.

"Yeah, yeah," said DJ. "Whatever you say."

Leo got married on a Saturday afternoon.

(Jay and DJ had received a joint invitation, which Jay was trying really hard not to get too worked up over. They lived in the same house, of course they got a joint invitation.)

The entire ceremony was bilingual - a college friend of Leo's officiated in smoothly simultaneous English and ASL, and Leo and his fiancé (now husband) Ryan both signed their vows as well as spoke them, for the benefit of Leo's largely Deaf extended family as well as Ryan's hearing one. Ryan's signing was still a little shaky, even to Jay's out of practice eye, but much more fluid than it had been the last time she'd seen him talking to Leo's parents. She had a feeling it was more because of nerves than anything else - after all, they were his wedding vows. His voice was shaking a little bit, too.

Jay thought it was sweet.

Without really thinking, Jay leaned over to DJ, resting her head on DJ's shoulder. "It's not fair, Deej."

"What's not fair?" DJ whispered back, sounding amused.

"They're so cute," said Jay. "Look how he's looking at Leo. *Our* Leo!" She shook her head, turning it slightly to rest her forehead against DJ's shoulder instead of the side of her head. "I want somebody to look at me like that, Deenie."

DJ chuckled softly. Jay felt her turn her head to look down at her. "Yeah, okay. You don't even date, Jazzy."

"I still want somebody to fall in love with me," Jay said. She lifted her head up to look at DJ and suddenly realized exactly how close together their faces were.

DJ was smiling at her, the kind of smile that's soft around the edges but carries pure amusement through the eyes.

The kind of smile that sets Jay's entire being on fire.

"It'll happen, Jazz," said DJ. Her smile quirked into something a little more wry. "And in the meantime, you've always got me."

"I do," Jay agreed.

DJ laughed again - more an amused exhale than an actual sound - and pressed a small kiss to Jay's forehead. "Good. Now pay attention. Your friend's getting married up there."

Jay turned her head back toward the boys, who were still vowing, but she left it resting against DJ's shoulder.

DJ's arm came up to wrap around Jay, tugging her a little bit closer.

"I'm happy for him," Jay said quietly. "Look at that smile, Deej."

DJ didn't respond out loud, just nodded.

For the reception, Jay and DJ were seated with the handful of their childhood friends who'd been invited - Jay was sitting between DJ and Mitch Garner, with Mitch's fiancée Annie on his other side, then Zac Garner, his boyfriend Brendon, Lizzie Poole, Dahlia Jennings, Nell's girlfriend Siobhan, and then Nell herself was on DJ's other side.

Jay was quietly but painfully aware that fully three fifths of their table was made up of couples, and there was a small ache in her chest wishing it were more.

Nell gave a speech, Siobhan holding her drink for her so that she could sign, since she was Leo's best woman. Leo and Ryan were at a little sweetheart table not too far away, looking sweet and sappy and in love. Ryan's best man spoke after her, from a table a little ways away from theirs with one of Leo's cousins interpreting for the Cruz side of the family.

It was a fun night, all told. Jay always loved getting together with their childhood friends, a strong thread connecting them even after growing up and growing apart some. Seeing Dahlia was different - she saw Dahlia all the time, since DJ and Dahlia were sisters. She came around more often, and they had dinner with the Jenningses moderately regularly. But the rest of them were harder to pin down, especially to get everybody in one place.

DJ had been convinced away from a dress, much to her mother's inevitable chagrin, instead wearing a green button-down with sleeves rolled to the elbow tucked into high-waisted dress pants with suspenders and a purple bowtie. She'd picked out Jay's outfit, too, because Jay didn't trust her own sense of style as far as she could throw it for an event like this, so Jay wore a light, flowy green dress that hit her legs about mid-calf. They looked good together, like a matched set. That made the ache in Jay's chest come back every time she thought about it, but she wasn't about to complain. If DJ wanted them to look like a pair then they were going to look like a pair.

(DJ had justified it to Jay by pointing out that any photos from the reception they were in would likely be of both of them, since they were rarely out of arm's reach of each other at Nolan's wedding. That they ought to look good together if they're going to be next to each other all the time anyway.)

Jay was struck, sitting next to DJ and across from Dahlia, by how little the twins looked like each other in that moment. Dahlia and DJ were fraternal, but for a long time growing up people hadn't quite believed them when they said so. And, sure, they bore a strong resemblance. They had the same narrow face and sharp jaw, the same straight nose and dusting of freckles, they were both taller than Jay by inches. But that was pretty much where the overlap stopped.

All dressed up, it was easy to see the differences. Dahlia's hair was lighter and fell in much looser curls, which she had swept back away from her face in an interesting sort of swirly updo. Her eyes were greyer, more like David's than DJ's, which were a clear summer sky blue. Dahlia had opted for a striking blue dress and a full face of makeup, which managed to even make her facial structure feel different to DJ's bare face. Jay had done DJ's hair for her, pinning it back so it was half-up-half-down with little sparkle pins in the part she'd twisted back, carefully arranged curls cascading over DJ's shoulder.

(DJ had clipped one sparkly pin into Jay's own hair, taming a lock of hair on the shallow side of her part that was making an insistent attempt to be in her face tonight.

"And now we match," she'd said with a fond smile. Jay had smiled back, her heart aching.)

There was food, which was pretty good, and DJ picked out all of her tomatoes and put them onto Jay's plate, which was almost hilariously normal on such a special occasion.

There was dancing, and it was actually Nell who dragged Jay out to the dance floor first, while Siobhan and DJ had a serious sounding conversation about pipe organs.

"You two are a pretty picture tonight," Nell said, twirling Jay under her arm.

"Yeah, well, you can thank Deej for that," said Jay, laughing. "She dressed me."

"Oh *did* she?" Nell teased. She wiggled her eyebrows.

"I hate you," Jay said without any heat. "I hate you so much."

"Hey, I'm not the one who waltzed in here on the arm of the girl I've been in love with since high school looking like *that* and playing cool about it," said Nell. "When are you going to tell her, Jay-Jay?"

"Never," Jay said, letting Nell spin her again.

"Jay -"

"Nell, no," said Jay. "Never. We're good, we're happy. We live together. I can't screw that up on a half-baked *chance* that she'll love me back."

"But she does, Jazz," Nell insisted quietly. "She does, and everybody in the universe can see it except for you."

Jay shook her head. "Nellie, she would've said something."

"You haven't."

Before Jay could formulate a response, somebody tapped her shoulder. She turned her head back, her eyes falling on DJ.

"Hey, Nellie, mind if I steal her back from you?" DJ said across Jay.

Nell's hands dropped immediately, and she gave Jay what she was sure was supposed to be a meaningful smile. "All yours, Deej."

Jay just about fell into DJ's arms, because she turned too fast and lost her footing, just as the song changed to something slower than before.

DJ laughed, because she laughed at Jay no less than twice a day, and caught Jay easily. "How come you can do all that fancy dancing with Nellie and as soon as I get here you're tripping over your feet, Jazzy-Jay?"

"Nell was leading," Jay said, laughing along. "I had to take that step all by myself."

"Well," said DJ, pulling Jay a bit closer with a hand on her waist, "I think I can take the lead, too, then."

She did, guiding Jay through the steps of their dance, leaving Jay to just stare up at her and think about what Nell said. *She does. And everyone else in the universe can see it except for you.*

What would DJ being in love with Jay look like?

Jay wasn't sure. All she knew was that she'd never seen a change in DJ, in the way she acted around Jay or the way she spoke. They had always been close, tossing casual friendly *I love yous* and existing in each other's space and things, and DJ had never in all the time they'd been friends given Jay any indication that she might have romantic feelings towards her.

Jay felt like she would know. She would have to know. She knew DJ better than anyone in the world.

DJ spun her out, then back in even closer to her.

Jay decided to stop worrying over whether or not Nell was right. She was going to just live in this moment, *enjoy* this moment, where the love of her life was holding her and they were having fun and it was their best friend's wedding and the whole energy of the night was light and happy and just buzzing with *something*.

"It's sort of wild," DJ said softly, "that Leo's married. *Married*. Like a proper grown-up."

"He is," said Jay. "We are. We're twenty-four, Deej."

"I don't know," said DJ. "I still feel miles away from being a real adult."

"I don't think it's as simple as that," Jay replied. She leaned forward, her head resting on DJ's shoulders. "You're not married, but you've got your feet under you as a musician. We've got an apartment that's all our own and we pay our own bills and buy our own groceries. We're in our mid-twenties, I think everybody this age is just improvising. I know Leo and Ry are, still."

"Well, I'm glad you're there to improvise with me," DJ said, and her voice was so soft and thoughtful that Jay actually picked her head up to look at her.

There was something, *something* in DJ's eyes. In the soft edges of her smile. Something fond and sweet and almost, *almost* like -

"There you two are!" Leo's voice cut in, through the hazy moment they'd been having.

"Leo!" Jay said, letting go of DJ to pull him into a hug. "Congratulations!"

"Thank you," said Leo. "And thank you for coming, I'm so glad we were able to get everybody here. It means the world to me that you came."

"Of course," said DJ, leaning down to kiss Leo on the cheek. "We're having a great time."

"I can tell," Leo said, grinning. "You look so much less like you want to die than you do in all the pictures from Nole's wedding."

Jay laughed. "Your insistence won out in the end."

"And I'm glad for it," said Leo. "I'll let you two get back to your dance, I just wanted to catch you at least once tonight."

"Congrats, again," said DJ. "You two have something special, hold on tight."

Leo nodded. He opened his mouth like he was going to say something else, then closed it again and just smiled at them before walking away.

Jay and DJ were staying in the hotel that hosted the reception that night, in a shared room. It had seemed silly to book separately. It had turned out when they checked in that their room only had one bed because of a miscommunication in booking, which was a little annoying but fine. They had shared before and they would certainly share again in the future.

All of this meant that Jay and DJ stumbled, tipsy, into their hotel room late, late that night, and once they'd changed into pajamas they wriggled under the covers of the same king sized bed. There should've been plenty of space for them to spread out, each with their own room to sprawl without being in each other's way.

But this was Jay, and this was DJ, and they gravitated toward each other like a comet to a black hole.

Jay wasn't surprised when she woke up the next morning draped half on top of DJ, one arm pinned underneath her while the other was thrown carelessly across DJ's middle, their legs tangled together under the sheets. Her head was pillowed on DJ's chest, and one of DJ's hands was resting just over Jay's hip while the other had found its way into Jay's hair.

It wasn't a surprise. But it still made Jay's breath catch in her throat, still made her heart light aflame.

It felt like a moment Jay had borrowed from some other version of herself, one who'd worked up the courage to actually say something about her feelings.

DJ's fingers scratched soothingly at the base of Jay's scalp. "You think too loud, Jazz. Go back to sleep."

"Sorry," Jay whispered back.

"Mm. Don't apologise. Just close your stupid eyes."

"So bossy."

"Tired."

"Right. Sorry."

DJ hummed sleepily. "Love you."

Jay closed her eyes tight, willing DJ not to notice the way her breathing changed at the words. "Yeah, Deej. Love you, too."

Fifteen: This Year

Jay honestly wasn't entirely sure how she had let herself be talked into this. Singing in DJ's videos was one thing, but - well.

Ever since DJ's Candlelight video a few years ago, they had been branching out more and more. People had absolutely *loved* the video for Candlelight; DJ had done a little intro explaining the song's origin and her surprise for Jay before she set the camera up for her ambush, and their viewers had fallen in love with her. There had also been a widely positive response to the feel of the part of the video where she actually sang the song, with the camera flipped to include Jay in the shot.

After testing the waters some, they had identified a few of the elements from that video that people liked which were easy enough to replicate:

1. People liked hearing the stories behind DJ's original songs; she started doing introductions for every video for a song she'd written, though the covers stayed music-only.

2. They liked the somewhat behind-the-scenes feel of it. Jay had put

together and posted a bloopers video a few months ago and it was, as of now, one of the most viewed videos on their channel.

3. They liked Jay. Jay herself couldn't fathom why, but DJ had taken this as an excuse to convince Jay to sing with her more often, and by extension she tended to appear in the behind-the-scenes and intro type segments more, too.

All of this had come together in the form of Jay sitting on a stool next to DJ in their living room, in front of their rearranged backdrop, in a St. Clare Chameleons t-shirt and a wig.

"Hey, guys!" DJ said to the camera, her hands in her lap. Her guitar was waiting just to the side on its stand. "Welcome back to, like, two thousand and ten."

"We're singing a song Dinah wrote when we were, what, fifteen?" Jay added. "And Deej thought it would be *real* funny to dress up as our high school selves to sing it."

(It kind of was, actually, but Jay wasn't about to admit to that.)

"It's worth it for that wig alone, Jazzy," DJ replied. She reached over and ruffled Jay's fake hair, before turning back to the camera. "If you guys can believe it, Jay had even longer hair than this when we were kids."

Jay readjusted her wig, which DJ had left sitting slightly askew.

"And if this wig has told me anything, it's that I don't regret chopping it off," said Jay, rolling her eyes. "It tickles my face, Deej."

These pieces to camera were always a funny balance between their actual personalities and a more exaggerated version of themselves that was a little more entertaining to watch. Jay was still getting the hang of it, but DJ was a natural.

"Deal with it, it's just a few minutes," DJ said, unconcerned. "Anyway, like Jay said, we're dressed as our fifteen-year-old selves! We dug out some of our old volleyball shirts - go Chameleons! - and we even swapped our backdrop around just for this."

"Yes, if you look closely you'll note that we switched out the painting of us as nineteen-year-olds for a photo of us as sixteen-year-olds," Jay added, a playful note in her voice. "The difference is striking."

"Shut up," said DJ, playing along. "This song is a fun one because it's a couple of firsts! It's the first song that I wrote that still feels like my music, and also the first song of mine that I ever wrote a harmony line to sing with Jay!" She grinned brightly and it was like all the air left the room, or at least Jay's lungs.

"It's still my favorite," Jay jumped in, also grinning. "Well, second favorite, after Candlelight."

DJ hummed, nodding. "Right. Of course."

"The song is called Golden, and it's about to be ten years old. It's honestly a little bit wild that she hasn't played this on the channel before, because this is the song that Dee has performed for the most audiences that aren't me," Jay said, doing her part for getting some information into this intro. "Dinah, you ready?"

DJ had picked up her guitar while Jay was talking, and she nodded. "Whenever you are."

Jay smiled at her. DJ started to play.

Jay hadn't been exaggerating when she said that this was the song

DJ had played the most out of all of her originals, and singing it with her came as easy as breathing. Even though she felt a little silly doing it in her high school volleyball shirt and a wig that kind of, almost looked like her hair before she'd cut it, it was easy. Natural.

There wasn't really a single thing in the world that Jay would rather be doing right now, either. She loved singing with DJ, especially singing DJ's songs, especially singing Golden.

DJ still wouldn't confirm or deny firmly that Golden was about Nell, even ten years later, but Jay would be surprised if it had come completely from nowhere.

Shocked, even.

DJ leaned into her a little bit when they hit the first chorus, throwing an easy smile her way.

"And we'd be golden, we'd be -

Jay smiled back, playful and light. They had sung this song together enough times that the call-and-response on the chorus feels familiar and warm, with a routine of movement woven into the music. *"You and me?"*

"We'd be golden," DJ finished the line, winking.

Golden was less wistful now than it had been when DJ was seventeen. No longer tinged with aching sadness, and instead more upbeat, a little brighter. Jay couldn't help smiling through the song, and she saw that same fond smile echoed on DJ's face.

It still faded a little bit though the bridge, but by the end she was smiling at Jay again.

"One more thing before we go," DJ said after a moment once the song was done. She flashes a bright smile at Jay, because heck *yes,* they'd gotten through this in a single fluid take so far. "We've had a lot of requests recently to do a little Q&A, and I finally got Jay to agree to be on camera with me for it!"

Jay rolled her eyes, chuckling. "She says that like I can ever really get out of doing these with her. We'll be filming it a week from today, Saturday, so from Sunday to Friday feel free to leave any questions you've got for us in the comments!"

"Feel free to ask about anything - music, songwriting, Jay's got some strong opinions about books -"

"I'm a *novelist,* of course I've got strong opinions about books. Somebody ask Deej about baby grand pianos if you want some strong opinions."

"Why are they called that?" DJ added helpfully. "Just give them their own name! They're full grown pianos, they're not going to get any bigger."

"All this and more," Jay said through a laugh. "Again, you have until Friday this week for questions, and until then -"

"We love you, thanks, bye!"

Jay couldn't help fully laughing as DJ turned off the camera. She was never going to get tired of DJ's signoff, which had originally been the result of a bit of a ramble in her first post-Candlelight video with a piece to camera, but which her viewers had found generally charming and Jay had gotten a kick out of, so it stuck.

"You think we'll actually get questions?" DJ asked, sitting back down next to Jay.

Jay shrugged. "Who knows. I think we might, though. This isn't the sort of thing we'd have come up with on our own; a lot of people were asking to see more of you."

"Of us, Jay," said DJ. "Of *us*." She reached over and ruffled Jay's wig again. "Thanks again for going along with this. You're always a good sport, I really appreciate it."

"Hey, it was fun," Jay admitted. She pulled the wig off, running her fingers through her own hair. "I don't miss the long hair, though."

DJ laughed. "I swear, you put that on and you, like, physically de-aged before my eyes."

"I think my face looks older than it did in high school," Jay protested. "Less round at least, thank God. I looked like a beach ball with the bob."

"No," DJ said, almost a whine. "It was cute!"

"It was not," said Jay. "Didn't suit me one bit."

"No, it didn't," DJ agreed, "but it still looked cute. You're happier with it short, though, and it shows."

"I am." Jay reached out to DJ with her foot, brushing her shin with her toes. "I really do love doing this with you, Deej, as much as I always whine. Your music is really important to you, and it means a lot to me that you let me in."

"My music wouldn't exist without you," DJ said, shrugging. "There's no one in the world I'd rather share it with than you."

They stared at each other for a while, content in the quiet. For just a single, breathless moment, Jay almost felt like they were sitting right on the edge of something, something important.

And then DJ's phone buzzed, and the moment shattered into little bits.

DJ reached for her phone, rapidly responding to whatever text she'd received, and Jay just watched her. Moments like this happened with increasing regularity, and Jay wondered, *wondered* what it was they were on the edge of.

She had a hope, a wish.

But it was unlikely and fleeting, and by the time DJ had shoved her phone into her pocket and turned the conversation to a dinner plan, Jay had balled that hope up and tucked it away in a deep, dark corner of her mind. No use dwelling on it if it wasn't going to come to anything, right?

For all that they were only doing this by request, DJ and Jay were both thoroughly blown away by the number of question submissions they'd received going into this non-musical Q&A video. Jay had spent most of her free time in the last few days picking through the comments for good questions and common questions - which mostly overlapped but not entirely - and making a list of the ones they'd actually answer on camera.

The number one most commonly asked question was -

Well, Jay wasn't looking forward to answering it, but enough people had asked that it would be weird if they didn't address it.

They settled on ten questions, time allowing, and set the camera up facing their couch like DJ had for Candlelight so they could be a little more comfortable while they answered.

"Okay, Deej, here we go," Jay said, pulling up the list on her phone. "First question: when did you start playing music and when did you start writing? I know that technically those were two questions but I saw both of them a ton and I figure you can answer them at once."

DJ lit up. She'd been really worried that this wouldn't pan out. "My parents have a piano, and I fell in love with it young. I started lessons when I was six, and then I picked up guitar on my own when we were thirteen or fourteen. I've been writing my own music since eighth grade, but the first few songs were not that good, and you will not be hearing them." She grinned. "It's Golden and later on this channel."

"We did The Coming Out Song for Pride last year," Jay pointed out. "That's pre-Golden."

"Right!" DJ said with a laugh. "That one got a pass, but the coming out song isn't *good*, it's just *fun*."

"Granted," said Jay. "Next question: does Jay play any instruments?" She looked straight down the camera. "No. And you should all be happier for it."

"That's not true," DJ countered, putting her hand on Jay's arm. "We learned recorder in fourth grade."

"First of all, if you handed me a recorder now, sixteen years later, I would definitely not still be able to play it," said Jay. "And second of all, even if I could, nobody in the entire world wants to hear my terrible, awful, fourth-grade-level recorder playing."

DJ snorted, but waved for Jay to move on.

"Alright, time for a small diversion!" Jay said. "This one isn't really a question, but it made me laugh: Dinah, baby grand pianos are called that because they look like grands but smaller, nobody's expecting them to *grow*."

"Jazz, have I told you recently that I hate you," DJ said without any heat at all. She turned toward the camera. "Look, guys, I *know*. But I still super hate it. Just call them something else! They're like ponies - ponies aren't baby horses, they're just small genetically! So we gave them a *different name*. All I'm saying is that with the entire English language in front of us, we could have done better as a society in the naming department."

Jay laughed, she couldn't help herself. She'd been on the receiving end of the baby grand piano rant more than anybody else in the world save maybe, *maybe* Dahlia, and it always amused her endlessly.

"Okay, okay," said Jay, reaching over and patting DJ's leg. "You good?"

"I'm *fine*," DJ said firmly.

"Next question," Jay said, looking back down at her list. "What was the first song that we actually wrote together?"

"Candlelight," DJ said, shrugging.

"That doesn't count," Jay counters. "We didn't collaborate on it the way we do now, our two pieces were independent of each other."

DJ chewed on her lower lip for a moment, before answering. "Then it was Sunset, wasn't it?"

"I think so," said Jay. She hums the end of the bridge to herself, trying to think of whether anything else had come first. *When all is done and through, at least I'll be home with you.*

"I should do that one on the channel soon," DJ mused. "Okay, what's next?"

"I've got one more music one and then a couple about us," Jay said.

DJ nodded. "Okay, neat."

"Don't bite my head off," Jay started, "but we got this one a *lot*. Why haven't you ever done any Christmas songs for your cover series?"

DJ frowned, her eyebrows crinkling together. It was January, and they'd seen this question on their videos all through November and December for the last three years. They'd answered it in their comments plenty of times, but people kept asking.

"I'm Jewish," DJ said flatly.

Jay shrugged at the camera. "Not everybody does Christmas, guys. We kind of thought that that one was obvious, but here we are."

"There are, like, a million other musicians on the internet singing Christmas music," said DJ. "I do not intend to join them."

"Hopefully this'll cut down on the number of people pestering you about it next year, though," Jay said with a pointed glance at the camera. She knew full well it wouldn't. She leaned on DJ, their arms aligned from shoulder to elbow. "You ready to move on?"

"*Please*," said DJ.

"The next set are going to be about us, like I said," said Jay. She was steeling herself. The first few were fine, but the last one she was sort of dreading.

"Shoot," DJ replied, smiling.

"Do we have day jobs?" Jay read off of the list.

"Like, at all?" DJ asked, clarifying.

"Yep," said Jay.

"Short answer yes," said DJ. She had turned half toward Jay, and she had a playful smile on her face.

"I work at a bookstore, and DJ teaches babies how to play piano," Jay explained. She did not roll her eyes, but she was extremely tempted.

"My youngest student is *six*," DJ corrected.

"Babies!"

"Shut up," DJ said playfully. "Do you have another question?"

Jay did, of course. "Tangentially related to the last one - did we go to college, and if so, what did we study?"

"We did both go to college," said DJ. "I studied music, both composition and education. If songwriting doesn't work out, I want to be a music teacher when I grow up." She winked at the camera.

"I did creative writing," Jay added. "Mostly focused on fiction writing, but there was some poetry, nonfiction, and screenwriting in the mix too. I'm deep in redrafting the novel I wrote my senior year, but I use the poetry writing more often day-to-day now that I'm working with Dinah most of the time."

"Any more, Jazzy?" DJ asked, tipping her head to one side.

"Yeah, I like the next one," said Jay. "How did we meet?"

DJ's entire face lit up. "Oh, that's a sweet one."

"I have to say, I am still baffled that people want to hear about me, too," said Jay, shaking her head. "I'm just along for the ride, guys, really."

"That's not true," DJ said, fully facing the camera again. "Don't listen to her, any of you. She's the reason you're watching this at all."

"Shh," said Jay. She reached over and put a hand over DJ's face. She was mostly aiming for her mouth but hit somewhere closer to her left eye. "Dinah and I met when we were in kindergarten. On the first day of kindergarten, actually."

"She gave me a nickname and declared us best friends forever, to my recollection," DJ said, pushing Jay's hand away and smiling fondly at her. It was the sweet, soft one that she always seemed to save just for Jay, and it made her little candle flame - always present, nowadays - flare up to warm her all the way to her fingertips.

Jay's cheeks were hot, too, and she hoped beyond hope that she was not visibly blushing.

"That's not how it happened," said Jay, shaking her head. "You were nervous because Dolly wasn't in our class, and I decided I wanted to make sure you had fun. I didn't declare us best friends forever for at least another week."

DJ laughed, bright and clear, and it made Jay's heart flutter. "Yeah, sure. Something like that. Either way, Jazzy-Jay has been my best friend for about twenty years."

"On the subject of Dolly," Jay said, purposefully looking away from DJ and back at her phone to try to calm her racing heart, "do we have any siblings?"

"Yes!" said DJ, smiling toward the camera. Her smile had widened into a brighter grin, less soft around the edges. "I have a twin sister, Dahlia. This channel was actually her idea originally! And then we have a little brother named David who makes me feel *so* old every time I remember how old he's getting."

"He'll be eighteen soon," Jay said, poking DJ's side and winning a theatrical shudder from her for her trouble.

"Eighteen!"

"I am the middle child of three," Jay plowed on, despite DJ's somewhat put on existential crisis next to her. "One older brother, Nolan, and one younger sister, Meggie. We're two years apart in both directions - Nole's already married and living his best grownup life, and Meg is in college still."

"Okay, last question, right?" said DJ. "This should be ten."

"Right, ten," said Jay. She took a deep breath, looking down at her phone again even though she knew what the question was. Even though it was burned into her brain. She looked up at DJ, forcing a playful smile onto her face. "This was the most asked question by *far*."

"Hit me," DJ said, grinning.

"Are you guys married?"

DJ's eyes went wide. "Wait, really?"

"Number one question by a *mile*," said Jay, laughing. "There were a few variants; how long have we been together, were we high school sweethearts, can we show some wedding photos in the video - it all shakes out the same, though."

"No," DJ said, not to Jay but toward the camera. She sounded slightly stunned. "No, we are not. We never have been - what - where did people get that idea?"

"I think it's because you call me your partner all the time," Jay guessed. And she did, pretty much any time she referred to Jay in an intro. "And we live together and stuff."

"Are you kidding me, guys?" said DJ, and the tone of sheer disbelief in her voice made Jay's heart sink until she added, "Jay is *way* too cool for me."

Jay laughed. "I'm pretty sure it's the other way around, Deej."

DJ shook her head, laughing. "Not true. Anyway, yeah, guys, no. We're not married. Not even together."

"Nope," Jay agreed.

"Is that everything, Jazzy-Jay?"

"Sure is."

"Great! Well, this was fun, let us know if you guys liked it!" DJ said toward the camera. "We'll have a regular music video up next week. Till then - we love you, thanks, bye!"

Jay got up and turned the camera off, then flopped back onto the couch across DJ's lap.

"That was really the most asked question?" DJ asked again, running her fingers through Jay's hair. The contact had Jay - who was feeling surprisingly frayed for how straightforward the whole thing had been - buzzing. She felt that candle flame feeling flickering under her skin from her scalp to her fingertips to the ends of her toes.

"For real," said Jay. "Can you imagine?"

"What, us married?" said DJ. She shrugged. "I don't really think it'd be that different from now, Jazzy-Jay. They had to get the idea somewhere."

Jay, privately, thought the same thing, that their imaginary married life and their current life would really only be different in a handful of ways. But that was a line of thought she didn't allow herself to follow often.

"Well, if your romantic prospects are still as hopeless as they are now in ten years, we can talk about it," Jay joked. "I'd marry you for the tax benefits."

DJ laughed, but it was lighter than before. "Aw, Jazzy, that's the sweetest thing anybody's ever said to me."

That was the last they talked about it, but it hung in the back of Jay's mind.

That was three weeks ago.

Sixteen: Now (Again)

Jay breathes for what feels like the first time in twenty years. She careens back into the moment, into her own brain, into *oh my god did DJ really just say -*

"Sorry, you *what*?" she says, her eyes wide as she takes in DJ. DJ who is sitting across the table from her, casual as you please, looking like she'd just said something about the weather and not thrown Jay's entire world off its axis.

"Love you," DJ replies, and it's barely, *barely* a breath. "I love you. Jay. Is that - is that okay?"

Jay just stares at her, uncomprehending. Her brain feels like it's short circuiting.

So much for DJ not being able to surprise her anymore.

"I'm sorry," DJ says, getting up. "I'm sorry, I shouldn't have - I made everything weird, I'm sorry."

"No," Jay chokes out, catching DJ by the wrist. She stands up, too. "No, Deej - don't apologize."

"Don't?" DJ echoes. She isn't quite meeting Jay's eye, and suddenly that is absolutely killing Jay.

Jay wants DJ to want to look at her. She wants DJ to mean this, she's absolutely *aching* for DJ to mean exactly what Jay thinks she means by *and I love you.*

She wants DJ to look at her with those gorgeous, clear blue eyes and say *I love you* again and again until the end of time. And if DJ backtracks now Jay is going to fall to pieces right here in their stupid living room.

"No," Jay repeats. "Because if you apologize, that means you want to take it back and I - I don't think I can take that."

"You *don't* want me to take it back?" says DJ.

Jay shakes her head silently. There is pressure building up in her head, her eyes are starting to prickle with the beginnings of tears, she can't *breathe*, she can't breathe, she can't breathe.

Her whole world has flipped on its side, but there is one thing anchoring her to reality and that one thing is *DJ, DJ, DJ.*

DJ loves her.

How -

How in the world could DJ love her without Jay ever noticing?

Jay knows everything about DJ. She knows the smile she gets when she thinks things are going to go her way. She knows the way her laugh sounds when she's faking it, but she doesn't want anybody to notice. She knows the way her face lights up when she sees someone she loves.

Jay has grown up with DJ. And in all of her life, she's never seen that light in her looking at *Jay.*

But here DJ is, standing in front of her with her own tears glazing over her eyes, telling Jay that she loves her.

"Jay?" DJ says softly. "Jazzy, say something?"

"What do you want me to say?" Jay says. It's the wrong thing to say.

"Anything?" DJ blinks, *hard*, and a little tear squeezes out of her eye, though it clings to her eyelashes instead of rolling down her cheeks. "Literally anything in the world, so I know I didn't ruin everything?"

"You didn't," says Jay. "You didn't, Deej." She takes a shaky breath. "Why?"

Jay has kept a subconscious running list of things DJ likes for a long time. It's a list that leads with *one word song titles*, but includes things like lace-up boots and buttoned shirts with silly patterns and satisfying harmonies and has ended with Jay since as long as Jay could remember. But to jump from the list that includes pancakes to the list of things DJ really, deeply loves - the list that starts with her family and probably ends with Johnny - feels almost earth shattering.

"I was just looking at you, and you were all sweet and happy and you made me breakfast and it just hit me all over again and I blurted it out before I could think," DJ says all in a rush. "I know - I know it's all just - and we've gone this long without - but I just, Jay. Jazzy, I love you so much and now that I've said it I don't think I'll ever be able to stop saying it."

Oh.

"Oh," Jay says, because she cannot find her God-blessed *voice*.

"You've been my best friend in the world since we were five years old, Jay," DJ says, and it seems like now she's going she can't stop herself from continuing. "Since we were *five*. And I figured out - God, Jay, I figured out what love felt like looking at *you*. I think every love song I've ever written has been about you. I know you - I know you've got your theory about Golden, but it's more complicated than that."

Jay opens her mouth to respond, but the words get lost. She closes it again.

How is she living in a world where she knows DJ better than she knows her stupid self, but she hasn't put this together?

But she hasn't *believed* when other people told her over and over and over?

"I've gotten comments asking if you're my wife since we first started the music channel and I swear to God, every time I see it it kills me a little that you aren't," says DJ. It kills Jay, too. "And I know that this must be weird for you, and I'm so, so sorry."

DJ pulls her arm out of Jay's grip, turning away.

"I'll - I'll get breakfast cleaned up."

"Deej!" Jay finally blurts. "Deenie, no, you've got it all wrong."

"What?" says DJ, frowning as she looks back toward Jay.

"DJ, Candlelight is about you," Jay says simply. It's not really what she means to say, but it does more or less get her point across.

"I - oh."

"Yeah."

"But you wrote it for that assignment," DJ says, her brow furrowed. "It wasn't supposed to be your voice."

"I wrote it the day I realized I was in love with you," Jay says, and as she does she realizes it's the first time she's actually said that out loud. "We were in your room and you sang Golden just because I pestered you into it, and you were just so - you were beautiful, DJ. You are. And it hit me like a ton of bricks, but at the same time I - it wasn't a surprise. And it was all I could think about, so I wrote that and I figured, hey, nobody will know if I hand this in for the assignment. And then he made me read it in front of the entire class and I thought I was going to *die*."

"You're in love with me?" DJ whispers hoarsely.

Jay nods. "And then you wrote the song for me, the melody, and I - I was almost sure you knew, for a while."

"I never did," says DJ.

"I know," says Jay. "I can see that now."

"You think I'm beautiful?"

"*That* can't be a surprise," Jay says softly. "I tell you all the time."

"I know," DJ says, a little distantly. "But it feels different to hear it now."

"I know," says Jay.

DJ stares at Jay for what feels like a long, long time. And then she says, sounding shocked beyond measure, "Say it again?"

"You're beautiful," Jay says, taking a step closer to her. She doesn't quite move all the way to her, there's still eighteen inches or so between them that feels like it might as well be an ocean. "Dinah, I love you."

"I love you, Jay," DJ replies, just a bare whisper.

Jay is pretty sure she's crying. It's not really an active thing, but she can feel tears spilling over her cheeks and she's pretty sure her last few breaths have been hiccuping gasps.

"Jay?" DJ says, moving just a hair closer. Her hand comes up to cup Jay's cheek, sweeping tears away with her thumb. "Jazz, what's wrong?"

"Nothing," Jay says, and she means it. "Nothing in the entire world. Deej, I love you."

DJ chuckles softly. "Oh, Jazzy, is that all?"

Jay nods. DJ moves closer still, leaning down to press her forehead to Jay's.

"This is going to sound so dumb, but I didn't figure it out until I played Candlelight for you for the first time," DJ admits.

"What do you mean?" asks Jay, lost.

"That I loved you," DJ says. "I didn't realize. I'd written whole songs about you, but it wasn't until I was sitting there watching you - singing a song with your words that I couldn't stop myself from writing - and I just went *oh, it's you.* Of course it was you."

"And you never said anything?" Jay says. She knows she has no room to talk, but - well, she can't help asking.

"Hello, Pot," DJ replies, rolling her eyes, "my name's Kettle."

Jay laughs softly at that. "Right, I know. Sorry."

"We're a matched set, really," says DJ. Her hand leaves Jay's face, but only so she can cup the back of Jay's neck instead. Her other hand comes up to join it, and Jay feels her lean a little bit of her weight onto Jay's shoulders, like maybe she's gone a little weak at the knee. "Disasters, the both of us. Do you know how much crap Nellie has given me over you?"

"At least as much as she's given me, I'm sure," says Jay. She brings her own hands up to DJ's waist, steadying her a little. "God, she and Leo are going to be insufferable."

"It'll be worth it," DJ says, and Jay cannot help but agree.

"Hey, DJ?" Jay says, lifting her head away from DJ's to get a better look at her face.

"What, Jazzy-Jay?" DJ replies with a soft, sappy smile. The one that makes flames dance under Jay's skin all the way to the tips of her toes.

"Would it be alright if I kissed you?" Jay asks. It suddenly feels like the most important thing in the world that their first kiss be right here and now. Nothing could possibly be more *them* than standing here in their living room in their pajamas, in the middle of the life they've been building together, caught up as ever in each other's orbit.

"I think I'd like that very much," says DJ.

Jay doesn't plan on keeping her waiting.

It isn't the neatest kiss of Jay's life. She misses the mark a little bit at first, and DJ feels a little taller than Jay expected her to, but none of that matters. What matters is DJ's mouth on hers, her fingers tangled in her hair, Jay's hands firmly anchored on DJ's hips.

What matters is that this is eight years coming - longer.

What matters is that Jay is finally, finally in her best friend's arms with no secrets left. She loves her, she loves her, she *loves her*, and she's not ever letting go, not for a million dollars and not in a million years.

Jay has had, technically speaking, better kisses than this first one with DJ. That doesn't matter, because they have the rest of their lives to improve their technique.

What Jay has not had - ever, not once - is a kiss that made her feel like she'd been set ablaze, candle flame flaring into a wildfire that she had no hope of putting out.

They separate, breathing hard. Jay touches her forehead to DJ's again.

It was nothing special, as kisses go. It wasn't long, really, or practiced or perfect.

But it was *Jay* kissing *DJ* and that is world stopping.

The whole thing feels new and sends sparks through Jay's whole body, but at the same time -

At the same time -

At the same time, it feels like coming home.

Jay steals another quick kiss.

She's never done this before, not with DJ, but it feels like she has. It feels like she's done this a thousand times, because this is *DJ* and DJ feels like home.

Jay is pretty sure that DJ *is* home.

"I love you," Jay whispers again, just because she can.

"I love you," DJ echoes, and it feels like the world has finally aligned to where it's supposed to be.

Jay doesn't know what tomorrow will look like. She doesn't know about the next day or the one after.

But she knows, knows with a deep, anchored certainty, that DJ will be right there by her side through it all.

And that, Jay thinks, is all she'll ever need.